"Cawdor, n

Cawdor had the guard down and the gun out of the holster before Jessie could cross the small distance of her cell.

"I don't care," Cawdor screamed back. "One way or another, I'm going to get that bastard for what he's done!"

"Walk out that door and you're a dead man," Jessie warned.

"I stay here and I'm a dead man," Cawdor answered. "Now, are you with me or no?"

* * *

SPECIAL PREVIEW!

Turn to the back of this book for a special excerpt from the riveting new Western by Gene Shelton . . .

Texas Horsetrading Co.

. . . A rousing epic novel of the Wild West from the acclaimed author of *Texas Legends*.

Available now from Diamond Books

— **WESLEY ELLIS** —

LONE STAR

AND THE
SLAUGHTER SHOWDOWN

JOVE BOOKS, NEW YORK

LONE STAR AND THE SLAUGHTER SHOWDOWN

A Jove Book / published by arrangement with
the author

PRINTING HISTORY
Jove edition / March 1994

ISBN: 0-515-11339-5

A JOVE BOOK®
Jove Books are published by The Berkley Publishing Group,
200 Madison Avenue, New York, New York 10016.
JOVE and the "J" design are trademarks belonging to Jove Publications, Inc.

PRINTED IN THE UNITED STATES OF AMERICA

10 9 8 7 6 5 4 3 2 1

LONE STAR

AND THE
SLAUGHTER SHOWDOWN

★

Chapter 1

Jessie let her gaze wander west, out past the fence to the fertile hills in the distance. In an hour it would be dusk, and it would take nearly that long to ride back to the house. Still, she could not help herself; the land, the pastures, the hills in the distance, they all held her with their beauty. Now, at this hour, when the cloudless sky was darkening, and the horizon turning bloody gold, she could understand why her father had fought so hard for the land. And she could well fathom why so many had died for land. Texas land.

"Do you see something?" Ki asked, spurring his mount to come up beside her sorrel.

Jessie raised the brim of her hat with a finger and turned toward Ki. The sun had cast his half-Japanese, half-American features in a warm glow. "It's beautiful, isn't it, Ki?"

"Yes, it is beautiful," he answered. "But we should start back. Finish tomorrow."

Ki's practicality yanked Jessie from her daydream.

1

He was right. They had started out early, determined to ride the length of the fence, yet now as dusk began to settle, they had not finished even half. It was not the first time this had happened and if they were lucky, it would not be the last. The chore, which most ranchers would be content to leave to hired hands, inevitably fell to Jessie and Ki. It was not that she did not trust hands to note the breaks in the fence and repair them, as Ki well knew. It was that she was determined not to let them have all the fun. Still, after all these years, a lifetime, she could not surrender an excuse to ride the perimeter of her land.

"Tomorrow, then," she answered, pulling on the reins to turn the sorrel.

Ki followed suit, but even as they pointed their horses home, they saw a long figure in the distance, dusting up the trail as he came.

"Briggs?" Jessie asked, turning to Ki. "Coming out to tell us that supper's waiting?"

Jessie's small joke was met by silence as Ki kept staring at the approaching rider. Instinctively, Jessie brought her hand down to the peach grips of her gun. As the rider approached, she saw clearly that it was not Briggs, and very possibly it was trouble.

When he was still a couple hundred yards off, the rider began waving. His hand waved furiously over his head as the words reached Jessie in only a weak murmur.

"Recognize him?" she asked. Worry was beginning to sink in. She could not place the rider, though she was sure he wasn't one of her hands. One of her men who rode a horse like that, practically to death at a full gallop, wouldn't be working for her long. She'd have him fired before the animal cooled down.

By way of an answer, Ki slid his hand slowly to the pouch where he kept the *shuriken,* the razor-sharp throwing stars.

The rider was nearly to them now, fifty yards off, as he spurred the panting, wild-eyed claybank forward. Now, she could hear him, his rasping voice nearly as winded as the horse. "Miss Starbuck! Miss Starbuck!"

Jessie let her hand rest casually on the Colt on her hip. If the need arose, she could clear leather in an instant, but somehow she doubted it would be necessary.

Ki urged his horse forward a few steps, as if to meet the frantic rider, but really to get within range for one of his throwing stars.

"Miss Starbuck!" the stranger said, pulling up on the reins and bringing the horse to a grateful stop in front of Jessie and Ki. "They told me to find you here. Just didn't figure it'd be so far."

"Who? Who told you?" Ki asked.

"Foreman, your foreman did," the rider, who was no more than a boy, replied while still trying to catch his breath.

"You shouldn't be riding such a fine animal that way," Jessie scolded. The horse looked about a foot from death and grateful to be there. Even now, at a full stop, it was still wild-eyed and trembling.

"Been riding like this all night, all day, almost," the lad answered, catching his breath some.

"Then you're lucky you're not walking," Jessie shot back.

3

"Got a letter, special letter," the lad offered. "Important letter."

"Let's have it then," Jessie said.

The lad fumbled with the reins as he began working both hands to unbutton his sweat-soaked shirt. When he pulled the letter out, it was as wet as the cloth of his shirt.

Jessie took off a calfskin work glove, reached out for the letter, then tore into the thick paper of the envelope. "It's from Malcolm Birnam," she said, not to the boy, but to Ki.

Ki knew the name well. Birnam had been a good friend of Jessie's father. They had come to Texas together, fought together, and built their lives together. Birnam's ranch was second to none, except, of course, the Starbuck spread. "Is it trouble?" Ki asked, worried now.

"Rustlers," the young man said. "It's bad. Killed three of our men couple days back."

Jessie, folding the letter, nodded her agreement with the young man's assessment. Though not as eloquent as Malcolm Birnam's plea for help, it was certainly to the point.

"Killed them like you'd kill rats," the boy continued. "Killed 'em like dogs. Then hung 'em up in a cottonwood. Shooting 'em, dry-gulching 'em with a Sharps, then running the cattle 'cross the river. You gotta help, Miss Starbuck. The hands won't ride out no more. They burned a man in a line shack. Nailed him into it, then burned it down. Soaked it in kerosene."

Jessie slipped the letter into her pocket, then looked over at Ki.

"We should ride out early," Ki said.

Jessie nodded. "Okay then, we'll leave tomorrow, before dawn."

"Thanks, Miss Starbuck," the lad said. "Mr. Birnam, he's in a fix. He said you'd come. Said it to me and a bunch of the boys."

"What's your name?" Jessie asked, spurring her horse forward, toward home.

"Maclean, Hardy Maclean."

"Okay then, Hardy Maclean," she answered. "You can bunk with my men tonight. Tomorrow we'll ride out early."

"Yes ma'am!" came the enthusiastic answer. "Mr. Birnam said you'd come, and damned if you didn't give it two thoughts!"

They set out before dawn the next day. Hardy Maclean's horse was in no shape to make the trip, so Jessie supplied the boy with a pinto gelding, which she supposed she could swap for the claybank when they arrived at Birnam's spread.

The air was sharp with morning chill as they closed the gate behind them and left the Starbuck ranch. They began the journey at a walk. Maclean, who was still jumpy and excited, spurred the pinto ahead on the smooth trail.

"What do you think of all this?" Jessie asked, turning to Ki and brushing a strand of her shoulder-length blond hair behind her ear.

"Birnam is a good man," Ki answered, not taking his eyes off the trail ahead. "If he needs help, then there is trouble. He is not the kind of man to ask for help he does not need."

Jessie nodded. She had been thinking the same thing. Rustlers were a fact of life in this country.

Almost a force of nature. They followed cattle as surely as heel flies or ticks. But at most they were usually just a nuisance. A rancher only needed the stomach and a few good men to end their thieving. The more cowardly ranchers hired regulators and didn't ask how the problem was eliminated.

Jessie spurred her mount forward and rode up alongside Maclean. The young man offered her a smile and slowed the pinto down to a walk.

"How many men does Birnam have now?" she asked pleasantly.

"Thirty—thirty-one, counting me," the young man answered. But then he quickly revised his count. "Damn, I mean to say twenty-five—er—I guess that's twenty-six. With me, I mean. Keep misremembering them others."

"Others?"

"Yes ma'am," Maclean said. "Sent out five two weeks back. Rode out after them rustlers and never rode in."

"They could still be out there, tracking."

"No ma'am," Maclean answered with conviction. "Found the horses. Found them dead. Ground staked at a camp, shot through the necks."

"They shot the horses?"

"Yes, ma'am," Maclean said with a nod. "We figured they left them there as a message like. Found them in the morning, sent me out in the afternoon, just after supper. Mr. Birnam, he told me to ride like hell till I found you."

Jessie, glancing over to her left, saw that Ki had ridden up alongside her. Ki nodded his head grimly, and she realized that they were in for some trouble.

They ate their breakfast of biscuits, jam, and jerked beef in the saddle. By noon they had stopped only once to water the horses. Jessie figured that they were making pretty good time. With only a little bit of luck, they would reach Birnam's property line before noon the next day and arrive at the ranch house by supper.

"Who does Mr. Birnam have in charge of the hands now?" Jessie asked. "Jacob still with him?"

"Mr. Jacob, he's been dead going on five years," the boy answered. "Died right though, in his sleep. Doc said his heart just gave out. Went peaceful like. Everyone just thought he was sleeping late. Don't know why; Mr. Jacob never slept late, not at all."

Jessie nodded slightly in belated respect for the dead. Jacob was a good man, the best ranch foreman around. A fair, tough man who wasn't afraid of hard work. Hands respected him, and so did Birnam. "Who's he got as boss then?"

"Mr. Glamis," Maclean said. "Came from up north."

"Afraid I don't know him," Jessie answered.

"Came in one day, 'bout a week after we put Mr. Jacob in the ground, and just stayed on," Maclean explained. "Came in with a herd of Mexican stock horses. Tough bastards, pardon my language. Part of the deal was he had to break 'em. Time he was done breaking 'em, he had the job."

"He a good man?" Jessie asked.

"Tough as them horses he brought in," Maclean said. "He ain't no Mr. Jacob."

"How's he different?"

"For one thing, he's married," Maclean said. "For another, he don't take to no joking. Not at all. They

7

say laughing to him sounds like blaspheming to a preacher. Can't stand it. Reckon it suits Mr. Birnam just fine."

"Doesn't sound like Mr. Birnam's type," Jessie said, remembering the rancher who would strip off his clothes and jump into a watering hole with the hands or have the cook bake up cakes and sweets for one of his men's birthday.

"No ma'am, not the old Mr. Birnam," Maclean said. "I don't look to be disrespectful, not of the boss and owner, but I reckon it ain't like you remember. Not at all."

They continued on in silence after that, each of them lost in their own thoughts. Jessie couldn't help thinking about what the young man had told her about Birnam. She had fond memories of the Birnam ranch. It was, for her, like a second home. Laughter filled the house and the hands were more like family than hired help. Young men often found a home at the Birnam spread. They would come to the old man with their troubles, and in Jessie's recollection, he never turned one away. What's more, she knew for a fact that more than once he had sold or leased a small piece of land to a hand who married and wanted to raise a family. And even then, Birnam was always there to help. The entire county was filled with children named after him.

And then there was Birnam's own family. His wife had died young, but he had a son: Cawdor Birnam. It was strange that Maclean didn't mention him. Cawdor had been as spirited as Jessie when they were young. And Jessie couldn't help but smile at the thought of him. They'd been children together and played children's games. When they were older, it was Cawdor Birnam who gave Jessie her first kiss. Even now, her lips tingled with the memory of that kiss, stolen under a cottonwood.

She wondered what Cawdor Birnam looked like now. She wondered what kind of man he had grown into. For a moment, she considered asking Maclean, but then she stopped herself. She would rather find out firsthand what time had done to Cawdor and if he was still as handsome as she remembered or if her memories were a trick of her mind. Then too, she was fearful. If Cawdor had taken a low road in life she would rather find out later than sooner.

They rode in silence for a long while, the time sliding by as slowly and smoothly as the landscape or the sun overhead. By the time Jessie was through with her musings, it was nearly dusk.

They found a creek by the low incline of a hill and made camp. If they managed to break camp before dawn, it would be an easy ride the next day.

After supper, with the horses watered, fed, and tethered, Jessie settled down into her bedroll. Once again, she found her thoughts returning to Cawdor Birnam and those carefree days so many years ago.

★

Chapter 2

The beginning of Birnam's property line was hard to miss. A small river, cold and clear, ran along the border. On the other side of the river were the first heads of cattle, heads bent to the grass under the noon sun.

"Reckon this is it, Miss Starbuck," Maclean said, as they crossed their horses cautiously over the stony bottom of the river. "In another two hours we'll be in Mr. Birnam's parlor, leastways, you'll be."

Jessie nodded in acknowledgment but didn't say anything. Once again her thoughts had turned to Cawdor and the stolen kiss under the cottonwood.

"You seem worried, Jessie," Ki said, riding up alongside her. "Are you thinking of Mr. Birnam's troubles or his son?"

The mention of Cawdor, spoken out loud, jolted Jessie out of her daydream. Of course Ki knew of Cawdor; there were few secrets she did not share with him. Yet, to hear Ki speak about that first, young love made her blush.

"I see," Ki said, noticing her color change. "But we should be attentive to Mr. Birnam's problems. Is that not wise?"

"Yes, I suppose it is, Ki," she answered.

In the hour and a half it took to put the Birnam ranch house in sight, they passed some of the finest cattle Jessie had seen. No wonder Birnam was the target of rustlers. His stock were well fed and well cared for. They had grown large and fat on the sweet grass. Jessie knew that such cattle would fetch premium prices across the river in Mexico, but more could be made with a little artful work by a man who knew how to change brands. Why then would the rustlers settle for less, kill for less, than they could get with a little more effort?

The Birnam house was just as Jessie remembered it: a large three story wooden structure, its gray paint weathered from the wind and rain. A white fence surrounded the yard, and a large corral stood just off to the side. The barn, behind the corral, was the same weathered gray as the house. The place was as neat and pretty as any you could hope to find.

Two hands abandoned their work lowering hay from the loft to come out and meet the three riders. It was still hot. The sun had not yet reached that place in the sky where the air cools and the shadows lengthen.

One of the hands wiped the sweat from his face and took the reins of Jessie's horse, while the other gathered the leather of Ki's animal in his gloved hand.

"This here is Miss Starbuck," Maclean said,

11

stepping down off the pinto. "Take good care of her animals."

"What you do with that claybank Mr. B. sent you out on?" one of the hands asked. "You gonna catch hell six ways if you ruined that animal."

"That's between Miss Starbuck and Mr. Birnam. Don't you worry about it none," Maclean answered, feeling the importance of the urgency of his mission.

"Damn it if nobody wants to do no work 'round here!" came a roar from the barn. "I just reckon that none of you sons of bastards care for the job you got!"

All heads turned to the barn as a large man with a full beard of red hair emerged from the shadows. He was waving his arms and yelling, cursing, as if it were the end of the world.

"Mr. Glamis," Maclean whispered to Jessie. "That's him I was telling you about."

Jessie watched as Glamis stormed toward them, still cursing, the full intensity of his anger aimed at the hands, but his eyes fastened on Jessie and Ki.

When Glamis was right in front of Jessie, he stopped cursing. "I reckon you're the one, that Starbuck, Mr. Birnam sent for."

"That's right," Jessie answered, meeting Glamis's gaze head on.

When Glamis saw that he could not outstare Jessie, he turned his attention back to the men. "Well, don't just stand there, 'cause you ain't getting paid double what you're worth to stand there trying to catch flies in your mouth," he hissed. "Get her horses walked, watered, and brushed down."

"Thank you," Jessie said, just to be polite.

"Nothing to thank me for," Glamis answered curtly. "I was against sending for you. Against it from the get. We ain't got no problems I can't handle right on my own."

Jessie didn't answer. Apparently they did have a problem he couldn't handle. But she had met this type of man before, all too often. He was the kind who would never admit he needed help and who would never ask for it, especially from a woman.

"But I figured if it gets that worthless son of a bitch Maclean out of my way for a few days," Glamis continued, as Maclean was walking away, "I figured it couldn't be all bad." And with that, he turned and kicked the boy viciously in the backside.

Jessie was about to say something, picking her words carefully, but then another voice began calling. "Is that Jessica Starbuck? I declare, she's grown into a proper woman," Malcolm Birnam boomed.

Birnam's cries immediately silenced the foreman and brought a smile to Jessie's face. Looking up toward the house, she saw Birnam, older than she remembered and perhaps spreading out some in the waist, but still the same man.

Jessie took a step toward the house and Birnam came bounding off the porch to meet her. For a man in his sixties, he was still full of energy. She could tell, just by the way he walked. When they met in the middle of the yard, Birnam wrapped his arms around her and lifted Jessie off the ground. "Why, I declare, you're bigger, but don't weigh half as much," he laughed, spinning her in a circle.

"Maybe you're just getting stronger, Uncle Malcolm." Jessie responded as he set her down.

13

Taking a step back, Birnam let his eyes meet Jessie's and said, "Not stronger, older, girl. That's what I'm getting, older. And is that Ki over there, standing 'round not saying anything?"

Ki stepped forward and shook hands with the rancher. The firm grip was enough to make Ki believe that Jessie was right. Maybe Birnam was getting stronger with each passing year.

"Now you y'all come on in," Birnam ordered in a friendly voice. "I got you two rooms and hot bath water."

Jessie wanted to say something. She wanted to get down to business right off, but she knew it was better to accept the old rancher's hospitality before bringing up the grim matter of the rustlers.

As it turned out, Jessie was right. Birnam wouldn't talk of his problems until he'd seen that both she and Ki had decent baths and had plates of cold chicken, biscuits, and okra in front of them on the polished wood table. Only then, under the wide beams of the dining room, would he talk about his trouble.

"I swear they're stealing me blind, girl," Birnam said, spearing a piece of chicken with his fork. "Not a week goes by but ten, twelve head turn up missing. And I'm not the only one. They're hitting every ranch in twenty miles."

"Sounds bad," Jessie said.

"Bad don't cover the half of it," Birnam replied easily. "A couple of the boys in the stockmen's association are talking regulators."

"What about the law? The sheriff a good man?" Ki asked.

"Good enough I suppose," Birnam answered. "Good

14

enough to keep peace on a Saturday night. But this, this here situation we got is something else altogether."

Jessie knew what he meant. She'd seen lawmen who were hell on payday hellraisers and crooked carpetbaggers, but didn't stand a chance against rustlers. As long as they stayed out of town, the sheriff could ignore the situation. More than likely, the rustlers were smart enough to spend the ill-gotten money far from where they stole it.

"Perhaps if we were to organize a posse?" Ki offered.

"Now, that's just what I was thinking," Birnam said. "Glamis, you met him, he's all for it. Filled with piss and vinegar, he is. Figure we got about a dozen, maybe fifteen men set to ride. All we need is a leader like."

"What about Mr. Glamis?" Jessie asked cautiously, already knowing the answer.

Birnam leaned forward in his chair. "Frank's a good man," he said in a whisper. "Good man with a gun, but he's a hothead. What I need is a leader. Someone to keep them in line. Truesday, you can stop that listening and bring in some more of that chicken!"

Almost instantly, the door opened and a young woman, attractive in a city sort of way, came through the kitchen door directly behind Birnam, holding a plate of chicken.

It wasn't until she set the platter down that Birnam began speaking again in a whisper. "That's Truesday Glamis, Frank's wife," he said. "They came as a kind of team. She cooks, he manages. Something about her, though, just rubs me wrong."

Jessie saw what rubbed him wrong in the woman's eyes. There was something like anger in those eyes that sent a chill down Jessie's spine. "Maybe you need a new team?" she asked.

"I'm getting old, girl," Birnam answered, still in a whisper. "Old and tired. Both of them do their jobs. These days, that's all I can hope for."

"Seems little enough," Jessie answered.

"All I can hope for is somebody who does their damn job and that thieves don't steal so much I won't have nothing to leave Cawdor."

The name brought Jessie up sharp. It was a reaction that wasn't lost on Birnam. He smiled broadly, mischief playing around in those old, still-blue eyes.

"How is he?" she asked, just to be saying something.

"Who? Cawdor? That who you mean?" Birnam teased. "I'd say he's around, someplace. Grew up bigger than you. Maybe not as much sense, I'd guess. Bookish type."

"Really?" Jessie asked.

"It's a fact," the old gent confirmed. "Don't mind telling you, I had plans for you two. Me and your daddy, we both did."

"Not too much turns out like we plan, does it?" she said, her voice touched by sadness for reasons she could not completely understand. Perhaps it was something to do with mention of her murdered father or maybe because life had taken so many unexpected turns.

"Not too much," Birnam agreed. "Not enough, anyways."

16

"Well, it'll be good to see him again, anyway," Jessie said.

Birnam smiled, hope burning dim in those kind eyes. "Anyway, here's what I figure," he said. "There's a meeting tomorrow morning, three biggest ranchers from the territory and their best men. If all goes well, you'll be riding out by afternoon. That's if you're up to it."

"You know I am," Jessie said, her voice determined.

Birnam shifted his head to Ki, who nodded with the same iron determination.

"Good then," Birnam said, slapping both hands on the table. "Now, if you'll excuse this old man, I got to take my afternoon lie down."

A moment later he was gone, walking now like an old man, up the rough-hewn stairway to the bedrooms upstairs.

He had not even vanished from view when Truesday swept into the room with an attitude of self-importance and removed the unfinished meal from the table. Jessie made brief eye contact with her, and once again the look sent a chill through her. There was something about that woman she did not like, not at all.

"What do you think, Ki?" Jessie asked in a whisper when Truesday Glamis had vanished.

"I think that a man who must whisper in his own house has much to worry about," Ki answered.

Jessie nodded in agreement, but before she could reply, the front door opened and the sound of boots came across the large entranceway.

Looking up, Jessie found herself facing Cawdor Birnam. For an instant, both of them remained silent and slack-jawed. Jessie, for her part, knew

17

what had caused the shock. Cawdor had grown into a fine specimen of a man. The curly blond hair now hung down to his broad shoulders. He stood better than six feet, and the blue eyes were still as clear as a mountain stream. After what the father had said about being "bookish," she had expected Cawdor to have grown into a slight, near-sighted banker type. But nothing could be further from the truth.

"Jessica Starbuck, as I live and breathe," Cawdor gasped, astonished, mouth still open.

But before he could say anything more, Jessie was out of her chair and running toward him.

He caught her up in his arms, much as his father had done, then lifted her under the arms, holding her up to get a better look. "Just look how you've all grown up," he said, studying her face with an intensity that made her blush.

"I could say the same about you," she answered, feeling his strong hands around her.

Then it was his turn to blush. "I s'pose I put on an inch or two," he said as he lowered her to the ground.

"A foot or two is more like it," Jessie said. "Last time, well last time, you had to—" But she halted, remembering how Cawdor had to raise himself up on tiptoe to kiss her good-bye.

"And is that Ki?" Cawdor blurted out, glancing over Jessie's shoulder.

When Jessie looked, Ki was already out of his chair and coming toward them. Jessie moved out of the way so the two old friends could shake hands.

It didn't take long for the three of them to get down to business. Cawdor went into the kitchen and came back with a coffeepot and three cups.

Jessie was anxious to hear what Cawdor had to say. Perhaps he had a better handle on the situation than his father.

"Well, there's not much to tell," Cawdor said, leaning back on a chair in the library. "Not much at all. They're skinning us, those rustlers. Skinning us bad."

"You tried to get at them?" Jessie asked, then took a sip of coffee. It was strong enough to cure heel flies, just the way she liked it.

"Took a couple of the boys out, more than once," Cawdor confessed. "Didn't even get close. They vanished, them and a dozen head, across the river."

"No tracks? No signs of butchering?"

"They're walking them out, along creeks," Cawdor answered. "Walking them downstream, upstream, can't tell. Couple head turned up across the river. Fella down south bought 'em. But can't blame him; he was just a fella didn't know what he was buying."

"And the others, the other ranchers, they want to bring in a regulator?"

"They're good people, good men, but they're hurting," Cawdor said thoughtfully. "Like Pa says, I don't believe they know what they're letting themselves in for. Not at all. But I've seen regulators work. Sometimes they get the right fellas, sometimes no, but I've never seen them bring back anyone riding upright in a saddle."

Jessie nodded thoughtfully.

"And Pa and me, well, we just don't want to see some fella come in and start shooting at strangers and pay for the blood. We're looking to see law done, nothing else, but nothing less, either."

19

Jessie knew what Cawdor was talking about. She knew that men like Malcolm Birnam could remember when there was precious little law in Texas. Law and justice, well, they were what all the fighting and the blood was about. That's what they had fought for in those early years. Men like that weren't willing to give up what they fought hard for, at least not without a fight.

★

Chapter 3

The three old friends talked long into the night. They had much to share and much to discover about one another. It was a pleasant evening, and the three parted company late, heading regretfully to their different bedrooms.

No sooner had Jessie stripped naked and slipped into bed than she heard a soft tapping on the door. "Yes?" she whispered, already knowing who it was.

The door opened a crack and Cawdor slid his head cautiously in. Jessie had not yet turned down the light and now she was glad for that fact.

"I saw the light," Cawdor began slowly, almost shyly. Yes, he was the same boy she remembered from her youth.

"Of course you did. I haven't turned it down," she said.

"Ah then," he answered and began to leave.

"Cawdor Birnam," she whispered.

The door opened again and he stuck his head tentatively back into the bedroom. "Yes?"

21

"Cawdor Birnam, if you leave now, I'll never speak to you again, forever," Jessie said, remembering the words from a threat she used as a young girl.

Cawdor slid into the room, closing the door silently behind him. "Now I wouldn't want that, would I?"

"I should say not," Jessie said, rising up in bed so that both breasts slid out from under their quilted covering.

Cawdor walked grinning to the bed. "No, I would hate that," he mused.

Jessie opened her arms to greet him.

Coming into her arms, he sat on the edge of the bed and leaned toward her. When their lips met, it was with a familiar and forbidden tingling. Jessie opened her mouth slowly and felt his strong tongue tease her own as her nipples hardened and rubbed tantalizingly against the rough material of his shirt.

When they at last broke reluctantly apart, she brought her hands down and began unfastening the buttons of his shirt to reveal the strong, well-muscled chest, then the flat washboard stomach.

He slid out of the shirt easily, bringing it down over his arms as he bent to kiss her breasts, raising each one gently in the palm of his hand in its turn. First the left, then the right. His tongue slid over her taut nipples, hardening each one more in the cool air. The warm moisture from his breath sent a chill through her.

Slowly, he rose so that she was nose to belt buckle with him. There was a moment of fumbling then, as each tried to work the buckle, then the buttons of his trousers, their fingers tangling and colliding awkwardly. Finally, when he got his trousers undone, he shucked them on the floor and slid,

22

barefoot and naked, into her bed.

He took her into his arms and held her tight. Already she could feel his hardening member against her soft, white stomach.

"It's been such a long time," she whispered, her full lips close to his ear. "I never knew, didn't realize how much I've missed you."

By way of answer, he eased away slightly, then turning Jessie onto her back, he began kissing the hollow of her throat. She could feel his shaft, hard and hot, brushing against the inside of her thigh. As he worked his way lower, his tongue playfully exploring her fine, firm curves, she felt his shaft slipping gradually down the inside of her thigh until it was brushing against the underside of her calf.

"Oh, Cawdor, that feels so—so delicious," she cooed, her slender fingers playing along his muscular back.

Soon he was at her stomach, his knowing tongue darting this way and that in its teasing fashion. It was now his tantalizing fingers that played and caressed her thighs.

Jessie let out a low moan, spread her legs wide, and drew her heels back as she offered herself up to him. She could feel the tingling moistness between her legs.

When at last he brought his mouth down to her silken patch, it was with utmost gentleness. His full lips grasped just a teasing patch of hair up near the top of her thatch, then released it. Again and again he repeated this, nibbling his way down one side, then up the other.

Eyes closed, she surrendered to his caresses as low moans escaped from the back of her throat. When at last he had worked his way to the center of her wetness, she could resist no longer and thrust herself up at him. But he was a skilled lover, withdrawing just enough to keep the delicious teasing going.

Soon, she felt his hot tongue caressing the inside of her thigh, working its way without hesitation to the center of her moistness once again. Then, it was in her, cleaving her with smooth, slow strokes that sent waves of pleasure racing through every nerve in her body.

Deeper and deeper he explored, until his wonderful lithe tongue could discover no more of her secrets, could extract not a single quivering pleasure more from her.

"Now, please now," she moaned.

And he understood. He understood that to wait longer would be senseless. Using both hands, she guided him up, holding him firmly around the waist as he rose between her legs.

Then, very gently, reaching back to tease him with just the tips of her fingers, she guided his manhood into her moistness. But Cawdor had one more surprise. When just the smallest bit of him was within her, he paused. He stayed like that for a long time—for what seemed like forever to Jessie— then slowly, so slowly, he let the full length of his hardened shaft sink into her.

When he was completely within her, he paused again, then slowly began to withdraw. Wave after delirious wave of passion washed through Jessie until she could take it no longer. When he was nearly completely withdrawn again, she rose up, almost violently, and engulfed him.

And he understood that, too. The time for slow

teasing and loving games was finished. Soon he was matching her every upward thrust with a filling downward penetration.

The old bed creaked and groaned under their lovemaking. The very house seemed to shake to the timbers. Jessie reached around, grabbing his hard back in her hands, and pulled him toward her. Soon, that was not enough. Letting her hands stray down his back, she grasped his firm buttocks in two hands and pulled him into her with all her might.

And then they were reaching their moment, their passion arriving at its peak together. Jessie let out a long, low moan as she felt Cawdor explode within her. She brought up her feet and locked her ankles around his back as the passion spent itself in one endless moment.

Resting in bed, feeling the sweat cool on their bare skin, Jessie, still flushed from their lovemaking, turned to Cawdor and said, "I can see you haven't wasted the time we spent apart."

The young man smiled shyly, then studied the ceiling for a long time before answering. "I reckon I read a lot."

"You can't possibly learn that from books," Jessie giggled.

"Sure you can. You just have to know the right ones to read," he answered seriously.

"Nobody could learn all that from books," Jessie retorted with confidence.

"You can from French books," Cawdor answered.

Turning on an elbow toward the young man, Jessie said, "Cawdor Birnam, you're just full of surprises! I didn't know you could speak and read French."

"I can't, not a word," he said.

And then they both laughed.

By the time Jessie woke, Cawdor was gone. She half-remembered the kiss he gave her before dawn as he left to return to his own room. Even in sleep, her lips tingled from it. And even in the morning, she tingled from their night of passion.

Washing and dressing, she made her way downstairs to meet the neighboring ranchers, who were already arriving. A few of the men stood in the large dining room, sipping cups of coffee. Others sat in chairs, talking in low, hushed voices. Cawdor was in the center, moving from man to man, greeting them somberly as if they were at a funeral, pausing only to give Jessie a sly wink as she slipped by the gathering to the kitchen.

The large room was empty, but amid the clutter and sputtering coffeepots, she managed to find a cup of coffee and a few biscuits to settle her hunger. By the time she returned to the dining room, still holding a half cup of hot, black coffee, the meeting of the stockmen's association was just getting under way.

"Now, this is what I'm telling you," Malcolm Birnam was saying. "I'm telling you that if you bring in a regulator, send for one like a mail-order suit, then you're gonna have trouble. Maybe not immediately like, but sooner or later it'll come back and haunt you."

"Can't be no worse than what we got now," one of the ranchers retorted.

"It is, Dobbs. It's gonna be worse," Birnam answered. "Worse by much. And you boys know what I'm talking about."

There was a general murmur of agreement, and Malcolm let a small smile play along his mouth. "Now, here's what I'm proposing—"

"Malcolm, we all know what you're proposing," another rancher, a fat one, interrupted. "You done proposed it before. And what I'm saying is, you can propose till hell freezes over, but we got to think beyond a posse. It didn't work in the past, and it ain't gonna work now."

Jessie sought out Ki, whom she saw standing back, in a corner. For an instant, their eyes met, and Ki raised an eyebrow in unspoken acknowledgment. Even if he'd heard her noisy lovemaking the night before, which he undoubtedly had, since his room was next to hers, he would never mention it. Ki, among his multitude of good traits, was fastidious about Jessie's private affairs. In turn, she kept her nose strictly out of his business.

Suddenly, while Jessie had been lost in her own thoughts, she heard her name being called. Malcolm Birnam was introducing her to the group.

The room fell silent, waiting for her to speak. All these men, waiting for her to solve their problem. Suddenly she felt very much like the tardy student who had not prepared for the day's lessons.

"And just what is this plan you have, Miss Starbuck?" the fat rancher was asking.

"My plan?" she asked back. Obviously Malcolm had told them she had a plan. Well, it sure would have been nice if he'd told her she was supposed to have a plan.

"Yes, Miss Starbuck, the plan," one of the other men insisted.

Jessie was about to speak, but before she could,

a voice over her shoulder broke in.

"I'll tell you what the plan is, and it damn well don't include no outside regulator," Glamis bellowed. "The plan is, we catch these sonsabitches and teach 'em what happens to those that rustle in this territory."

Jessie turned as Glamis brushed by her, striding defiantly into the center of the room.

"And just how do you propose to do that, Mr. Glamis?" one of the men asked. "You've had your chance before. We all have."

"Not together we haven't," Glamis said. "We ain't taken our shot at them bastards together. I've ridden out after them with my boys, and you fellas have, too. But we ain't never have gotten all together like on this deal."

A murmur of agreement sounded around the room.

"Now, here's what I'm proposing we do," Glamis said.

The men hunched closer. Jessie glanced over her shoulder and saw Truesday standing in the doorway of the kitchen, hands on her hips, watching grim-faced as her husband explained his plan.

The strategy could work, from what Jessie heard. It included all the ranchers, ten or twelve of them, each assigning three men to the posse. They'd station the men up and down the river and the streams that fed it, waiting for as long as it took. Nobody guessed it would take more than two weeks before the rustlers hit again. And, if they didn't strike by then, the ranchers would relieve the old men with new. It could work, Jessie supposed. What troubled her, however, was that all the men would report to Glamis and not one of the ranchers.

"Well, what did you think of our little meeting?" Malcolm asked Jessie when the group left.

"His plan could work," Jessie answered. "I only wish you'd told me I was supposed to have something figured out."

"Wish Glamis had told me he had," Birnam said. "But he wanted the glory, I suppose. He's young enough to want it. Trouble is, if his plan don't work, he ain't gonna be able to show his face for a spell."

"It will work, don't worry about that!" a voice behind them broke in.

Turning quickly on her heel, Jessie found herself face to face with Truesday. She was holding a coffeepot and smiling. "More coffee, Miss Starbuck?"

"Thank you, no," Jessie said.

"No thank you, Truesday," Malcolm seconded.

When she had left, Jessie turned to the old man and said, "Something about her, I just don't trust."

"She's a good enough cook, better than average, I reckon."

"I didn't mean her cooking," Jessie answered, watching the woman retreat into the kitchen.

"I know," Malcolm said. "I may be old, but I ain't that old. That's why I want you and Ki to ride along, unofficial like."

"You think there will be trouble?"

"I don't know what it's gonna be," Birnam whispered back. "With Frank Glamis in charge, it could turn into anything. I just don't want it turning into anything that ain't legal."

"Ambush?" Jessie asked in a whisper.

The old man almost said something, but then changed his mind. "You and Ki, you two just keep an eye out. Don't talk to nobody but me. You got that?"

"Yes, sir," Jessie said.

"And darling, be careful," Malcolm said. "You see something that ain't right, just come back and tell old Malcolm. We can deal with it together."

It took a while, but the posse was ready to go before noon. Guns and supplies were loaded and men accounted for. The way Glamis was barking orders and arranging the men, it looked to Jessie like a full-scale military campaign. There were thirty men in all, each one heavily armed.

Jessie didn't like the looks of it. She'd seen posses before and had ridden with more than a few herself. But there was a meanness about this group. Given the chance, she was certain, Glamis would take the law into his own hands.

There was one tense moment. As the men were pulling out, Glamis rode back and approached Jessie. "There ain't no need for you and that friend you brought to ride along. You know that, don't you?"

"I know it," Jessie said, meeting his stare, which was more of a challenge than anything else.

"What I mean to say, we got enough hands," Glamis tried, the challenging stare now covered over by a look of concern. "We could maybe be a week out there. You might want to think about staying back, nice warm bed, fine food. Get Cawdor to stay and keep you company. He's a fine young man. Not like his pa, but still a fine young man. Nothing that a little backbone and a good woman couldn't cure."

"That's nice, but I'll ride," Jessie replied easily.

"Might be a week, maybe two," Glamis warned. "Hard couple of weeks. Living out of our saddlebags."

"I'll take my chances," Jessie said.

"Well, Mr. Birnam wants you in on this. I ain't gonna go against him."

As they filed out the gate in twos, Jessie, riding stirrup to stirrup with Ki, looked over at him. "What do you think?"

"This will not be good," Ki answered grimly. "Not at all."

Jessie didn't have to ask what he meant. Setting her eyes forward, she spurred her horse ahead.

★

Chapter 4

They rode for the better part of the morning at a steady pace. Jessie looked over the men carefully, judging their worth in a fight. Most were no more than boys, hired hands, paid thirty dollars a month, with room and board. They sat easily in their saddles, joking quietly among themselves, every now and again offering Jessie a curious backward glance. She supposed that most were probably grateful for the break in the routine of ranch work.

But for Jessie, the task ahead offered no such rewards. If she were right, they were looking at a gang of a dozen, perhaps as many as two dozen. And probably a good many of them were hard cases. They had killed before to protect their rustling enterprise and their necks, and no doubt they would kill again without hesitation. Jessie knew all too well that an instant of weakness in the face of such men could mean the difference between living and dying. She just hoped that the posse knew it.

The plan was simple enough. They would post a man every three-quarters of a mile or so along the river that abutted three of the property lines. All but eight of the horses would be returned to camp. Without the horses, they would be able to conceal themselves better, yet, with the horses that remained, the eight best riders would be able to pursue the rustlers, should that become necessary. The distance—that three-quarters of a mile—was far enough away to cover a good portion of the river, yet close enough to summon more men quickly. At the first sign of trouble, the men would converge.

The men began falling away from the group in late afternoon. By nightfall, all but Jessie and Ki had concealed themselves in the brush, each outfitted with a canteen and enough provisions for three days of careful eating.

Jessie and Ki would take spots far upriver, while Glamis was at the opposite end. Cawdor was dead center. By arranging themselves this way, they would be able to spread their leadership and experience out along the entire line.

Jessie knew it was good planning, yet she could not help but feel a little pang of remorse at being situated so far from Cawdor. No doubt, she would find herself under the stars, wanting the blond, well-muscled young man near enough to warm her bedroll and tickle several of her fancies.

Jessie found a hiding spot by the side of the river. A large fallen tree trunk provided the perfect abutment for a crude lean-to shelter. By spreading a small length of canvas along the fallen tree, then covering it with leaves and grass, it looked like nothing so much as a slight mound of earth from as close as twenty yards.

At dusk, one of the younger men rode up, driving a half dozen horses ahead of him, asking to collect Jessie's horse. "No need to worry 'bout nothing Miss Starbuck," he announced. "Another two hours, she'll be eating chopped straw and oats in one of Mr. Birnam's stalls. Fresh hay and smooth lumber all 'round."

Jessie gave the animal a final pat along its neck and settled down for the evening. Ki, who was the next posting back, would no doubt be doing the same. She had spent countless nights on the trail, many of them alone. She knew herself well enough to know that it wasn't loneliness that bothered her now. There were times when she thirsted after solitude. No, it was two things that put her on edge. The first was the task that lay ahead, which could take a few hours or a few weeks. And the second, which was harder to admit, was her reluctance to give up such a talented lover so soon after just discovering him.

The first night was a moonless one and it passed slowly. Jessie, like the others in the posse, ate a cold plate for fear of tipping the rustlers off by a fire. The food seemed tasteless, and she found herself strangely weary just after eating, but it was long after supper before she allowed herself to drift into a light sleep.

When she awoke, it was to the sound of hoofbeats. In the gray of the early dawn, she rolled slightly,

34

silently, bringing up the revolver from her side. Peeking out the edge of the lean-to, she saw Glamis riding up.

"Morning, Miss Starbuck," Glamis said as he raised two fingers to his high-crowned hat. "Mighty fine little dirt house you built for yourself."

Jessie stretched, uncocked the pistol, then crawled from her lean-to. "Morning to you," she said, blinking in the cool morning air.

"We'll be sending a boy down later to relieve you, that is, if you take a notion to wanting to tidy yourself up a bit. That is, if you don't take it personal and all."

She didn't know if all the men had the same option, but she excused the offer anyway. She didn't want to chance any special treatment, not from these men. As she did so, Glamis tipped his hat and rode on.

Even in exchanging a few words, she noticed there was something about Glamis that had changed. Some quality about him had shifted strangely within him. Somehow, he appeared to ride just a little taller in the saddle. His face was set just a little harder and meaner. He seemed to her just a touch more self-assured, as if separation from his wife or perhaps assuming leadership on this ride had strengthened him in some peculiar way that she could not quite define.

The next night only a sliver of a moon shone in a clear, star-filled sky. An odd feeling came over Jessie just after midnight. Stretched out in the crude lean-to, her gun within easy reach, she found herself checking the load, once, twice, and then three times. She told herself she had jitters, as if she'd drunk too much coffee too late at night.

An hour later, she heard the first bass grumblings of cattle. Just one or two mingled in with the night sounds and the creek's own soft music. They could have been strays that had broken through the fence line in search of water, but Jessie knew they weren't.

The sound of approaching cattle grew louder. She judged them to be downriver. Crouching now, the top of the lean-to against her back, the peachwood grips of her .38 in her hand, she waited.

She didn't have to wait long. An instant later, all hell broke loose. First came the sound of a muffled shout. Then a curse followed by gunshots.

Jessie bolted out of the lean-to and ran, keeping close to the edge of the river. Before she'd traveled fifty feet, four more shots rang out in the night. Then she heard splashing.

The bank of the river curved upward, and Jessie jumped into the knee-high water at a run. She stumbled once, her boots slipping on the slick rocks, then took off around the bend in a high-stepping run, splashing up water as she went.

Around a bend and seventy yards downstream, she saw them. A half dozen men on horseback emerged from a small herd of cattle. The men were bringing their horses around, guns raised, as more than twenty head bolted heavily, first one way, then the other.

As the men broke from the small herd, Jessie took position in the center of the river, determined to face down the rustlers. A few more shots rang out, scattering the frightened cows. Then Jessie saw the posse, spashing their way downriver. Someone had a lantern, the yellow light splashing up from the water as the man holding it zigzagged through the shallows uneasily.

The men on horses bolted, firing back over their shoulders as they scattered. More shouts filled the air, and the cattle rushed toward the riverbanks. Then the man with the lantern fell, and the flame died as a dozen gunblasts lit the darkness.

Two more lanterns appeared behind the chaos and more shots rang out from the riverbanks.

Three of the men on horseback fell, shot in the back, and the others spurred their horses onward, slapping down their reins across their spooked horses' necks as they swiveled in the saddle to trigger off a shot toward the posse at their backs.

It wasn't until they were just a few yards off that they spotted Jessie. Two of the rustlers brought their horses up fast; the third came up with a pistol.

Men were firing from the banks and from behind the rustlers. Jessie felt hot lead cleave the air by her head and ducked. Two more rounds plunked into the water at her feet. The posse was driving the rustlers toward her, threatening to gun her down in the crossfire.

Jessie fired twice, knocking the pistol-wielding gunman from the saddle as the two others split directions. Jessie broke left, going after one rustler, as a dozen men ran toward them.

She caught him at the riverbank, his horse complaining and straining to make the climb up the steep side. Running beside the horse and rider, she grabbed the rustler by the gunbelt and pulled. For

37

an instant she was dragged alongside the climbing horse, his hooves inches from her boots. Then the gunman fell, coming out of the saddle, cursing and tumbling at the same time.

Releasing his belt and stepping back, she let gravity do the work for her. The rustler hit the ground with a thud that knocked the wind from his lungs and the hat from his head as his horse vanished uphill into the brush.

A split second later, Jessie was on him, straddling his chest and pointing the cocked .38 up under his nose.

"Don't even blink," she ordered. "Not a damn twitch out of you."

"You got it, lady," the rustler said as he seemed to deflate slightly under her weight.

Jessie heard more shots behind her, then the sound of Glamis barking orders. Only when it had quieted down did she get off the gunman and order him to his feet. Then, very carefully, she marched him back down the hill and into the river.

The rest of the posse were finishing up. In the center of the creek was Glamis, still on horseback, supervising the operation of herding the cattle back together. A little way upriver, eight or nine bodies were spread out on the bank. Next to them, a member of the posse was in the process of unloading another body from across a saddle. The body came off the horse heavily and splashed into the water. The man cursed and dragged the rustler's body up on the muddied shore.

Glamis noticed Jessie for the first time, and he rode over and tipped his hat. Jessie noticed, right off, he was smiling. "Miss Starbuck," he offered, as cordial as you'd please.

"Where are the prisoners?" Jessie asked.

"Far as I can tell, you're holding a gun on all of them," Glamis said, still smiling.

"All dead—well, damn!" the prisoner in front of Jessie said. "Now that ain't right. No way you can tell me that's right. It just ain't right." And for the first time, she noticed he was barely more than a boy.

Glamis ignored the rustler, keeping his attention on Jessie. "S'pose it's a good thing you managed to capture one," the foreman said. "Got some questions I'm just burning curious about. Ask my questions, hang 'im, and I figure we can be home for supper."

"You can go to hell, fastest way, you son of a bitch," the prisoner said.

It took them the better part of the morning to clean up the mess. Several of the rustled herd had been hit by stray gunfire and had to be destroyed. A few cows had died in the river, and it took two men to pull them out.

When the heavy work was nearly completed, the owners began to arrive. They came up to the water's edge on buckboards and open carriages. A few brought their wives or nearly grown children to view the carnage. All of them packed suppers.

"A damned mess," Birnam said, viewing the carnage from his buckboard. Beside him sat Truesday, her mouth twisted into a mean little smile.

"Well, it's over now," Jessie answered, standing near the wagon.

"All but the hanging," came a voice at her back. Turning, Jessie saw it was Glamis. He was smiling broadly and wiping his hands down the front of his pants.

"How many?" Birnam asked.

"Killed ten," Glamis answered. "One prisoner, thanks to our Miss Starbuck here."

Jessie was going to say something about how all the men were shot in the back, but held off. She'd get her chance to speak with Birnam later without Glamis or his wife looking on. It seemed to her that more than one rustler should have been captured. If done right and proper, they could have brought in the whole bunch of them for a trial.

"Well, then, let's ride back," Birnam said as he started to turn the wagon. "Gonna have a party tonight. 'Spect that's in order."

"Yes, sir," Glamis beamed, and set off to cleaning up the last of it.

By the time Birnam's buggy had vanished over the hill, one of the stable hands was leading fresh horses to the men. The bodies had long ago left for town, piled like cord wood in the back of a wagon. Not surprisingly, all of the men waited for the return of their horses.

"What you thinking on, Jessie?" Cawdor asked on the ride back. They were moving at a walk, stirrup to stirrup.

"Thinking about how there didn't need to be so much killing," Jessie said.

"Hell, it's a miracle we didn't ride back a man short," Cawdor answered, smiling. "Wiped 'em out just like a nest of rats."

"There was another way to do it," Jessie retorted, angry at his mood.

Suddenly Cawdor's mood changed. The smile vanished into a little bit of nastiness. "And what way is that?" he asked. "If you don't mind my asking, that is?"

"The right way," Jessie said. "The proper way."

"Jessica Starbuck, you'll never change, will you?"

"And just what is that intended to mean?"

"Ever since we were little, nothing was ever good enough," Cawdor answered. "Nothing. We stopped the rustlers. You can't deny that, but you can move that pretty jaw to make noises about how we did it. Now that beats everything that I ever saw, heard, or been told about."

In answer, Jessie spurred her horse ahead, bringing him up to a graceful trot until she was riding next to Ki.

"That's right, Jessie, you just run away!" Cawdor called behind her. "Just like you always did!"

"Cawdor Birnam is displeased," Ki said, tactfully.

"Let him be displeased for all I could care, damn him," Jessie answered.

Ki made no reply. Among his many virtues, discretion was perhaps one of his best.

"Let me ask you something, Ki," Jessie said, speaking in a low voice.

He nodded slowly, already knowing what the question was. They had not spoken since the shoot-out, both too busy with their assigned jobs, but she had caught a glance from him several times. It was a look that meant something had gone wrong—very wrong.

41

"What did you think about that whole show?" she asked.

"It did not go well," Ki said. "Much confusion. Too much shooting. With patience, the men could have been captured, all of them, alive."

Now it was Jessie's turn to nod in agreement. "You were downstream. What happened?"

"Glamis," Ki said. "Glamis happened. He ran out, behind the men and cows. He fired the first shot. No warning. The herd stampeded. And then it was confusion."

"Notice that most of the men were shot in the back, at least once?"

"Yes," Ki said. "These men, they were rustlers, not killers. Two that I saw didn't draw their guns. I saw one man, his hands above his head, giving up. He was shot in the back."

"I guess we'll need to talk with Birnam, once we get back," Jessie said.

"Yes, that would be good," Ki answered. "But I doubt it will help. Even if he listens, he may not be able to do anything about it.

"But we have witnesses," Jessie said. "The others saw it as well."

Ki smiled. It was a small, sad smile. It said all Jessie needed to know. That one smile told her that men surrender glory reluctantly. The story would be one of valor on the part of the posse members. Folks might be quick to strip glory off another, but surrendering your own was like asking a banker for a loan. She knew as well as Ki that nobody surrenders glory easily. Already they were retelling the tale among themselves. By the time they reached the ranch, the odds would have favored the rustlers.

"We have another witness," Jessie replied.

"He will tell the story," Ki said. "Then they will hang him."

★

Chapter 5

By the time they reached Birnam's ranch, the party was already beginning. The other ranchers had brought whiskey and enough food to feed an army. Long tables were set up at the side of the house and the women had strained their lumber with steaks, chickens, biscuits, corn, vegetable stews, pies, cobblers, and fresh bread. Barely an inch of the long tables was left empty.

Jessie and Ki led their horses back to the barn and bedded them down for the night. Walking slowly around the house, they could already hear the noise. Someone had brought a fiddle and someone else was playing a mouth harp. It was dusk, and lanterns stood at the ready, meaning that the party would go on as long as it took.

Jessie had no appetite, none at all. It amazed her how these people could eat after such a slaughter, but eat they did. They ate and drank and danced. These were the winners. The losers were behind the barn, sheets covering their bodies. The one survivor sat tied and gagged off to the side, forced to watch the celebration.

Leaning against the side of the house, Jessie watched with mute disapproval. One of the ranch hands passed by and pushed a cup of corn whiskey at her. She didn't refuse. Maybe liquor could get her through the spectacle.

Twice Cawdor approached and asked her to dance, and twice she refused the offer. Both times he walked away, mildly drunk, to dance with a buck-toothed redhead whom Jessie took to be one of the neighboring ranchers' daughters.

When everyone had just enough to drink, the lanterns were lit and the speeches began.

With each speech the praise for the posse, particularly Glamis, grew more and more lavish. Each time, inevitably, Glamis's name drew shouts and applause from the audience. Finally, all it took was one drunk cowboy to get up and shout, "Glamis! To Frank Glamis!" to earn the applause and approval of the crowd.

Again and again, Jessie toyed with the idea of finding Birnam and explaining the situation, but each time she caught sight of him, he was slapping Glamis on the back, congratulating him.

It was after midnight when Birnam himself got up to make the final speech. The crowd hushed into a drunken murmur as he silenced the fiddler and halted the dancers.

"I suppose you all know why we're here," Birnam said. "Hell, we all been celebrating enough. Maybe some of you are too damn drunk to remember."

"Glamis!" someone yelled.

The crowd roared its approval.

45

"That's right," Birnam said. "Mr. Frank Glamis stopped the rustlers. It was his plan and his leadership that halted them sons of bitches."

"Damn right!" someone yelled drunkenly in response.

"He's a good man," Birnam continued. "That's why I'm sorry to say he ain't gonna be working for me no more."

The crowd hushed, shocked. Jessie leaned away from the house. Could it be that Birnam recognized the truth of the slaughter? No, she thought, that was too good to be true.

"And the reason he ain't working for me no more is that on behalf of myself and the rest of the stockmen's association, we're giving him a piece of land. Fifty acres to homestead with full water rights and grazing rights to the finest pasture land in Texas!"

The crowd roared its approval.

"I don't mind telling you, this boy's been like a son to me," said Birnam. "Aside from my own son, he's the only kin I got. And I'll tell you truthful, I couldn't ask for none better!"

The crowd shouted again.

Out of the corner of her eye, Jessie spotted Truesday. She was standing at the back of the kitchen door, frowning. Odd, Jessie thought, you get your own spread and can't do better than a tight-lipped frown.

By the time Jessie was shaken from her train of thought, Glamis was up in front of the party-goers giving a speech. Then he was shaking the hands of the stockmen as they handed over the deed to his new spread.

Jessie didn't have to wonder where Ki was; she

already knew. Twenty minutes before, she'd seen him and one of the servants, a young brunette, heading into the back door of the house. Well, it was a celebration of sorts and even if Jessie couldn't abide the reason for it, she couldn't deny Ki his fun, either.

"Ki, it was so good of you to help the men in the posse and all," the girl, whose name was Rosalie, said. They were walking toward the upstairs bedrooms.

"It was an act of friendship, of loyalty," Ki said, following her.

They had left the party a little while ago. The girl, who Ki discovered was twenty-one, was to give him a tour. He did not object, even though he knew the Birnam house from years ago. What he secretly hoped was that the tour would not stop with the house. And, by the way she was holding his hand, he had every reason to believe it would not.

"Isn't this just the most beautiful place!" Rosalie exclaimed. "Just beautiful." She sighed.

Ki looked at her in the hall lights. Yes, it was a beautiful house. Much love and patience had gone into its building. But Rosalie was a sight as well. Slim, with a heart-shaped face, and dark brown hair that matched her eyes, she was a vision. "Yes, it is beautiful," Ki answered. "But you are more beautiful."

The girl blushed and let out a small giggle. "Why Ki, if I didn't know better—"

"You would what?"

"I would think just the most awful things," Rosalie answered. "I would think that you were flattering me to gain my affections."

47

"If flattery is true, then yes, I was flattering you," Ki answered. "And, if you're asking if I would like to gain your affections, I would, very much."

Rosalie had stopped, just to the right of a large closet that held blankets and sheets. Cocking her head to one side, she said, "Do you know what I believe?"

"What is that?"

Reaching out slyly, she opened the door a few inches. "I do believe you talk too damn much." And with that, she slipped into the closet.

Ki quickly followed, but no sooner had he stepped into the large closet, than he bumped into Rosalie. She giggled again, then shut the door, plunging the small room into darkness.

Reaching out, Ki felt the young woman's hair between his fingers. A moment later, their lips met in the dark and they kissed passionately.

Ki circled her with his arms, drawing her to him. His strong arms held her tight in the darkness, while his hands gently explored her thin waist, firm buttocks, and solid legs beneath the layers of clothing. He could smell her; the scent was of perfumed soap and the food she'd prepared that day.

"Ki, oh, Ki," she moaned, breaking away from his kiss as her small dove-white hand worked its way up the inside of his thigh to where his hardened member throbbed urgently. She giggled again, giving his shaft a playful squeeze in the palm of her hand as she backed away a half step.

Ki wasted no time. Bringing his hands back around, he set to work on the fifty or more buttons that closed the front of her dress. Bending to her, he gently kissed each new inch of exposed skin that his efforts revealed. And with each button's release, she gave his manhood another squeeze.

When at last his kisses and caresses progressed down her lovely throat and chest to reach the lacy underthings, he slipped the dress gently from her shoulders. The calico material whispered to the floor and she stepped out of it.

"Ki, I'm afraid you have me at a disadvantage," she whispered, nuzzling into his strong chest.

For a moment, Ki didn't know what she meant, but he was soon to find out. The smooth shoulders and silken hair sank down, down, down, as her hands trailed teasingly along his chest. In an instant, she was working on the buttons to his pants. When she finished her work with the buttons, she reached inside, and he could feel the smooth flesh of her hand working the shaft out of the opening.

Outside the door, people passed by, unaware of what was taking place in the darkened room. Voices and feet on the wood planking advanced, then retreated, as Ki and Rosalie continued their amorous love play in total darkness.

Ki leaned back against the shelves of sheets, blankets, and quilts, then felt the warm wet touch of her tongue. For just a moment the velvety tongue lingered at the top of his shaft, the very tip of it drawing small circles. Then, without warning, Rosalie opened her mouth and took his entire length into her.

Ki suppressed a low moan as she allowed his member to linger in her mouth. Then, very slowly, she began to move her head back, inch by inch, exposing the moistened member.

Reaching down, Ki ran his hands through her hair, as she supported the shaft with one hand, the tips of her fingers playing a gentle tattoo across its base.

Once again she moved her head forward, taking him into her as her busy tongue and fingers teased him in patient pleasure. Then she was moving faster, the shaft burying itself deep in her mouth, then withdrawing. Each time, he found himself on the verge of crying out. Only fear of detection kept him silent.

Holding his wet shaft in her hand, she withdrew her mouth and rose slowly off her knees. Ki shifted position slightly, bringing his back to the door. Then, grasping Rosalie around her slim waist, he lifted her up and set her down on a small pile of quilts on the second shelf.

Her arms reached out and she grabbed him around the neck, locking her fingers just above his shirt collar. A moment later, he felt her legs encircling him, Rosalie's slim ankles hooking themselves at the small of his back. Reaching forward, Ki pulled her undergarments down below her knees.

Then, very gently, he moved closer, one hand holding his member as he guided it into her.

With the first touch of his warm, slick member against her downy patch, she let out a small, gasping moan and buried her head against his well-muscled chest.

Slowly, inch by inch, Ki worked his shaft into her. With each of his movements forward, she wiggled forward to meet the slow thrust, until, finally, he was buried deep inside her.

He rested then, feeling her moist warmth surround

him. Then, very slowly, he began to withdraw. When he was no more than halfway out, her ankles tightened at his back and she pulled him back in. Soon they were working together, the slick shaft moving slowly in and out of her warm, wet womanhood.

"Oh, Ki, Ki," she purred. "That feels so—"

Again, boots sounded just beyond the door and he shushed her.

She giggled a little and he began working the shaft faster. In a matter of moments his hardened manhood was sliding in and out of her with abandon. And each time the footsteps beyond their darkened closet came closer, each caught their breath in the excitement of being discovered.

Finally, suppressing a low groan of desire, Rosalie slid toward Ki, her firm bottom coming off the shelf. For just an instant, she began to fall, her locked ankles losing their grip behind Ki's back. Then he gathered her to him, his strong hands catching her up under her firm buttocks as they reached their moment together.

Rosalie nestled into Ki, her hands gently massaging his hairless chest.

"I do believe I have never—" she began to whisper.

But Ki shushed her again. Voices and the sound of footsteps approached once more. Then they stopped just outside the closet door. Ki and Rosalie held their breaths, waiting for whoever it was to pass. But they did not pass. They lingered there, just inches from the amorous couple.

"Pretty good, huh? I told you the old man would come through for us," a man's voice said in a drunken slur.

"Pretty good my ass," a woman's voice countered. "If you think I came out here to this forsaken place to live in a hovel, then you must be a crazy man. Crazy man."

"You'll see, I won't build us no hovel," the man, whom Ki now recognized by his voice as Glamis, said. "Gonna be a nice place. Cozy. You'll see."

"Nice place," the woman, who was unmistakably Truesday, sneered. "What could be nice that you could build? Three rooms with a dirt floor and mud walls? Cooking on a hearth like some—some pioneer?"

"It won't be so bad," Glamis cajoled. "And—and in a couple years—"

"Couple years my sweet ass," Truesday spat. "Now, be a man for once. You know what you gotta do. You know as well as me what needs to be done. So do it quick."

"I just don't know—not at all—" the man stammered.

"Do it and do it quick!" Truesday snapped, then stamped off down the hall.

"Damn, just damn it all," Glamis sighed to himself, then walked slowly away.

It took a few moments for Rosalie to put her clothing right, not an easy task in the dark. When Ki opened the door, he saw the look on Rosalie's face was one of total incomprehension. And he had no doubt that it was a look that exactly mirrored his own.

"I best be going," she said, stepping out of the closet.

"Yes," Ki answered, still thinking over what they had heard from their darkened hiding place. "That would be wise."

She kissed him once, lightly on the cheek, then turned quickly and headed down the stairs. He noticed that she moved light-footed, almost in a skip, and without a glance back toward him.

Ki waited, slowly counting to ninety in his head, then followed. He would have to find Jessie and tell her what he'd heard. Something was definitely wrong.

Moving cautiously down the wide stairway, he saw that the party had ended. The music could no longer be heard from outside, and the laughter that only a short while ago had echoed throughout the big house was silenced. He rebuked himself for losing track of time as he made love with Rosalie. For what had seemed like a few minutes of pleasure was obviously much longer. Those bootsteps in the hall that had heightened their pleasure by fear of discovery were the guests retiring for the night.

As he entered the main hall, his suspicions were more than confirmed. Most of the ranchers, or those who did not make it to their rooms, were passed out from brandy and whiskey. They sat asleep in the deep leather chairs, snoring loudly. Fat cigars were burnt to gray ash in ashtrays at their hands. The fire in the large hearth, stoked for the night, had died into a gentle glow. Someone had thoughtfully left the lamps dimmed, should any of the men awaken in the middle of the night in hasty need of a door. Blankets were spread out across their laps and pillows under their heads.

Ki turned, his first thought to alert Jessie. If Glamis and Truesday were planning something, then it was best that she know about it immediately. She would not mind being awakened or interrupted from her own amorous adventures to hear such news.

Retreating from the sleeping men, he moved back toward the stairs. But before he could take two steps, the world went bright white, like looking into the sun, then turned as dark as the closet he had just left with Rosalie.

★

Chapter 6

Ki dreamed he was drowning, plunging into a warm river so that the water flooded his mouth and nose. And then he awakened, drowning, fighting for breath.

Blinking open his eyes, he found himself soaking wet. The back of his head hurt so badly it felt as if the local blacksmith had mistaken it for an anvil.

"Ki, come on, it's bad," Jessie said, as the man who'd splashed water on him from a wash bowl vanished.

As he regained his senses, he noticed the men running. The sound of boots and yells echoed through the house. And farther off, outside, was the sound of horses.

"What has happened?" Ki asked, slowly getting to his feet.

"Birnam's dead," Jessie said, anxiously. "Come on, we got to ride."

"Dead?"

"That rustler came in and slit his throat before stealing a horse."

"Dead," Ki repeated numbly.

"That's who must have knocked you cold," Jessie said. She was checking her gun, turning the cylinder, and carefully checking each gleaming cartridge. "Let's ride then. He couldn't have gotten too far."

Just outside, riders were galloping away from the ranch.

Ki shook his head once, trying to clear it. Then he raised his fingers to his temples. "Yes, let's go."

In no time at all they saddled their horses and rode into the darkness.

"Did you see anything, Ki?" Jessie asked.

"No, but—" Ki began.

"He killed the man guarding him," Jessie broke in. "Strangled him with a length of wire."

"Jessie, I heard Glamis and his wife talking," Ki said. "I think they may be involved."

"I thought the same thing," Jessie answered. "Let's just wait and see how this comes out."

Across the pasture lanterns bobbed and weaved as the search party ran forward. If the rustler made it to the trees, then finding him would be hard, almost impossible.

But by the time they reached the tree line there was still no sight of him. Most of the men were still drunk and riding was hard. Jessie and Ki galloped ahead, racing toward the path that led toward the river.

"Where is Glamis?" Ki asked.

"He was the first one out," Jessie said. "Took off cursing and yelling like a banshee. Probably a quarter mile ahead."

When they reached the trees, far ahead of the others, Ki dismounted his horse and handed the reins to Jessie. Jessie nodded him on and he vanished into the tree line. If anybody could track a man in the dark, it would be Ki.

It took more than an hour on foot before Ki picked up the trail. Even then, it was tough enough. Horses and men had trampled every inch of the pasture to the tree line in search of the rustler.

Ki drew a *shuriken* from the pouch on his waist. He could hear the shouts of the other searchers in the distance as they crashed noisily through the brush and along the trails. He knew that the men were young ranch hands, excited at the prospect of the chase. If the rustler was nearby, they would be easy enough to avoid. They kept their lanterns lit and even far off, Ki could see the yellowish glow bouncing through the trees.

Ki stalked silently through the trees, blending into the darkness. He had gone maybe three-quarters of a mile before he heard the shot. It was close, just off to his left. Running soundlessly to the noise, he saw two figures. One was standing against a tree, hands clutching his stomach. The other stood a few feet away, holding a gun. Ki could not make out the faces. Either the wounded man or the one holding the gun could have been the rustler.

Throwing star firmly gripped, Ki stepped out from behind a tree a few yards from the men and shouted, "Stop! Stop there!"

The man with the gun spun around quickly and Ki let go with the *shuriken*. The gunman's finger came back on the trigger as the throwing star found its

57

target deep in the gunman's right arm. Ki ducked and rolled as the bullet sailed by his head. Another star already in his hand, he came up in a crouch.

Then the gunman did the strangest thing Ki could imagine. He turned back toward the wounded man, who crouched over in pain, and shot him again. The wounded arm did little to impair the gunman's aim, and this time the bullet hit its mark dead center of the wounded man's head, sending brain and bone splattering against the tree behind him. For an instant, the wounded man stayed crouched, then he fell over to reveal the debris on the tree behind his head.

"Stop there!" Ki shouted again. As the gunman started to turn, Ki sent another *shuriken* whistling through the air.

The star hit the gunman low on the chest, drawing a cry of pain from him as the gun fell from his hand.

Ki leapt forward to retrieve the gun as the killer fell to his knees. It was only when Ki was nearly to the revolver that he saw that the wounded man was Glamis.

Looking up at Ki, Glamis said, "Damn it, Ki, didn't you see it was me?"

"No, I only saw you turn on me," Ki answered as he stuffed Glamis's gun in his pants. "Then I saw you shoot at me."

"Well, he almost got away, thanks to you," Glamis said, holding his wounded arm as he tried to stand. "But I figure I got him."

"The rustler?" Ki asked, helping Glamis to his feet.

"Damn right the rustler," Glamis moaned. "Caught

him myself. Confessed to all of it."

"Before he died," Ki stated flatly as he looked back at the dead man. A Colt revolver lay near the body.

Men were crashing through the trees toward them, shouting and swinging lanterns.

"Over here! We're over here!" Glamis shouted.

A second later the first man arrived. He looked at Glamis, then at the dead man, and finally at Ki.

"You got him, boss," the man proclaimed. "But who got you?"

"Had a little mix-up is all," Glamis said.

Ki pulled the stars from Glamis's arm and chest, extracting a low moan from the foreman.

More men arrived, each one wanting to know what happened. And with each retelling of the story, Ki came out more foolish. In the final versions, he was nearly as bad as the killer. Then, finally, Jessie arrived and the dead man was tied over a saddle and the hunt called off.

It was nearly dawn by the time they all returned to the ranch. Jessie had not talked to Ki on the ride back, for fear of being overheard. But once they were back and the horses bedded down for the night, she drew him aside far from the ears of the other men.

"What happened out there, Ki?" she asked, speaking in a whisper.

Ki waited for a long time before answering. "I watched as Glamis shot the rustler," Ki said. "I was perhaps confused. But there was no fight between Glamis and the rustler. The rustler had no gun."

"You mean he just put that boy against a tree and shot him?"

59

"Yes, that is what happened," Ki said. "Stranger still, he did not speak after I wounded him. He turned back and shot the boy again. Very strange, is it not?"

Jessie was about to say something, to agree with Ki, when the sound of the pump broke the silence. Walking around the corner of the large house, toward the back, they saw Truesday. She was pumping mightily at the well, filling a bucket of water.

They watched intently until the wooden bucket was filled, thinking that she would haul it inside for cooking. But instead, she lifted it up as best she could, then poured it over herself. She had obviously intended to empty it over her head, but the filled bucket was too heavy and slipped from her grasp, spilling down the front of her dress.

Cursing, Truesday positioned the bucket under the pump and began working the handle again.

Three times she filled the bucket and three times she poured its contents over herself. When Jessie and Ki felt they had seen enough, they walked out toward the front of the house.

"Very strange, no?" Ki asked.

"Very strange, *yes*," Jessie answered.

"I think you should talk to Cawdor," Ki suggested. "I think you should do it soon."

"That's exactly what I was thinking," Jessie answered.

The Birnam funeral wasn't like anything the county had ever seen before. The death of the rustlers had brought out the ranchers, but the death of the great old man attracted even more people. They came on horseback and by buggy. The train depot, two days' ride away, unloaded passengers. And all the time, old man Birnam was arranged neatly in a casket filled with ice and flowers.

By the time the service was to take place, Birnam had been dead for nearly four days and the house proved too small. Six men carried the hand-carved casket outside and set it on a pair of black-draped water barrels. Those who could not find seats stood. And everyone was quiet out of respect, but perhaps more out of shock that such a man could die. It was not every day, nor every decade, that a man like Birnam died, and so easily at that. An era had come to an end with the murder.

The preacher spoke first. He spoke simply and slowly, letting the words sink in. Then came a long line of folks with the need to tell their stories. And the stories were sweet indeed. Each tale elevated the dead man to new heights of charity, bravery, and intelligence. By the end of it, the murder of the man seemed an event that would be told in New York, Chicago, and Philadelphia.

But in the end, Jessie knew that Birnam was, after all, just a man. He had lived honest and brave in the best ways he knew how. He practiced charity and compassion when it suited him and sometimes when it didn't suit him so well. And in the end, Jessie knew that was enough for any man.

When the speaking was done, the same six men loaded the box with the corpse and melting ice into a ranch wagon and started off for the grave. It took some time for everyone to reach the spot out in a far pasture. Once they were all assembled again, the preacher said a short prayer and a young girl sang a long hymn. Then they put Birnam into the ground.

The ride back to the ranch was one of quiet whispers and small, sad smiles. A few of the women had stayed back at the ranch to cook, and by the time the funeral party returned, every table in the house was laden with hams, chickens, pies, vegetables, and steaks. Huge pots of coffee steamed on the kitchen's stoves and children, wearing their Sunday-best on Thursday, ran in and out the doors. Above it all, organizing the event like a church social, was Truesday.

Several times Jessie tried to approach Cawdor, but each time she was eased aside by a neighbor or friend offering sympathy and the promise of help. Well, no matter, Jessie thought to herself. She could talk to him later.

But later never came that day. The guests didn't move to leave until after dusk, and many stayed for the night.

The next day was the reading of the will. Jessie, oddly, found herself invited, though it was supposed to be for family members and hired help only. And it left Jessie asking herself which category she fell into. Perhaps it was simply a gesture that Cawdor felt compelled to make.

The large library was filled with people by the time she entered. The judge, somber in his black frock coat and muttonchops, began reading the document in a sonorous voice. All around the room was the held-breath expectancy of what each would get.

The ranch, the land, and all of the estate went to Cawdor. Every ranch hand received fifty dollars in gold. So did the house help. And then came the provision that if something happened to the son or if he was unable to keep up the ranch, the entire estate would go to Glamis.

The words hit Jessie like a blow. It was a surprise, but it shouldn't have been. Hadn't Birnam himself said that Glamis was like a second son? Still, Jessie could not shake the feeling that something was terribly wrong.

Had Glamis known about the will? Probably. In a fit of good cheer, and no doubt filled with enough whiskey to make him benevolent, Birnam probably showed the will to Glamis. The old man had probably shown it to him never suspecting that he'd die in such a way. But Jessie knew exactly what it meant. By including Glamis in the will, he could not have done more to ensure his son's death if he'd put a price on his head. In fact, that is exactly what he had done.

Jessie let her eyes shift over to Ki, who stood stone-faced by the door. He knew, she surmised. Ki wasn't a fool; he must know! Yet he showed nothing.

As the men and women left the room, exchanging small nods and smiles, Jessie hastened over to Ki. "We have to talk," she whispered urgently.

"Yes, there is no time," came Ki's answer.

Together, they left the house and wandered out by the barn, far from any of the remaining guests. Jessie leaned against the wall. She didn't expect it to be a long talk, but she was already wearying of the subject. "Well, Ki, are we thinking the same thing?"

"I fear that perhaps we are," Ki answered. "And if we are correct, then Cawdor is in great danger. We must waste no time in warning him."

Jessie looked off, toward the house. Every light

seemed ablaze inside. The sound of people talking reached them as a faint whisper. "I don't see how he'd do it," she said. "I just can't see how he'd plan it out."

"Or she," Ki corrected.

The idea brought Jessie up short. Yet, the moment Ki said it, she knew he was right. Truesday had to have been the one who killed old man Birnam. Thinking about it, the scheme made perfect sense. She slit the old man's throat while her husband released the captive rustler.

"You do not believe she killed him?" Ki asked. "That she could kill him?"

"Yes, I believe it," Jessie answered. "It makes sense. Perfect sense, Ki."

Ki nodded, grateful that they were in agreement, though from past experience he had learned that they were usually in complete agreement on most important matters.

"Only thing I can't figure out is how they plan to kill Cawdor," Jessie said. "I mean, it would seem obvious, so soon afterward and all."

"I feel that with these people, nothing is obvious," Ki answered. "Particularly with Truesday. She is not an obvious woman."

"That's true," Jessie said. "But still, just to kill Cawdor for the land, why, every judge and federal marshal in two hundred miles would descend on them. They wouldn't stand a chance of making a claim. None at all."

"Let us watch for a while longer," Ki suggested. "But you must warn Cawdor. Warn him quickly. I fear, now more than before, that his life is in danger."

"I know the feeling," Jessie answered with a grim nod.

As they started back for the house, they saw a figure come down the back stairs. Stopping in the shadows of the barn, Jessie and Ki watched as Truesday once again went to the well and pumped a bucket of water. When she had finished her task, she began washing. Using a large slab of soap, she washed every inch of her arms and legs, then started on her face. She scrubbed furiously. And when she was finished, she kicked at the bucket viciously, sending its soapy contents spilling out over the yard.

★

Chapter 7

Jessie waited until the house was quiet before leaving her bed and walking silently down the hall to Cawdor's room. She opened the door as soundlessly as she could and stepped inside. The room was inky black. Close by, she could hear Cawdor's steady breathing as he slept.

She knew she would have to wake him sooner or later. But before she could make another move, the breathing stopped and she heard the sound of a hammer clicking back.

"I'll just fire until I hit something," Cawdor said. "So you best not move, not at all."

"Cawdor, it's me," Jessie answered, feeling both panicked for herself, and relieved for Cawdor. At least he knew that something was wrong—knew it enough to sleep with a gun in bed.

A moment later there was a scratch and a match ignited, revealing Cawdor, sitting on the side of the bed, still holding the .44 Colt. "Jessie, if you don't mind telling me what are you—" he began to ask, but before he could finish, the match burned down. He let out a hissed curse and threw the burnt stick of wood to the floor, sending the room back into darkness.

A second later, he'd lit another match and touched it to the lamp wick. The room glowed a warm yellow. Jessie took a step forward.

"Now, if you don't mind, how 'bout answering my original question?" he asked.

"I came to warn you," Jessie said. "Something isn't right. Not at all."

Cawdor made a small face that dismissed Jessie's assertion in a minute. "The old man's not in the ground a full day and you're creeping around telling me something's wrong? Is that what I'm supposed to take as gospel?"

"Take it whatever way you see fit," Jessie shot back. "But I'd say sleeping with a gun in your own house isn't a sign of confidence that everything's the way it should be. So, let's just start there, about why you've taken to sleeping with a gun."

Cawdor, realizing that the gun was still in his hand, thumbed the hammer back down and set the gun on the night stand. "No, I can't say I disagree," he said. "Don't want to admit it, but I can't help feeling someone's after me."

Jessie took a few steps to the bed and sat down next to Cawdor. "I think it's probably Glamis," she said. "Fire him now."

"Can't," Cawdor answered simply. "I fire him now, he'll take most of the hands with him. Won't be able to bring the cattle in."

"Do it," Jessie said. "Soon."

"It would look bad, too," the young man continued. "The whole state knows how my father felt about him. Everyone knew it. Even if he is dangerous, he can get me just as quick off the ranch as on. That doesn't mean I like it, but it's a fact."

It was a fact, but that didn't mean Jessie had to like it, either. "We'll do this then," she said. "You just stay close by—close as stink on manure—to Ki and me."

Cawdor hung his head. "Jessie, that won't work, either," he said. "You can't stay on for more than another couple days. I know it, and so do you."

She was still thinking about what to do when she heard the footsteps. Two men, both in boots, headed down the hall toward the room.

She waited, hand on the butt of the .38, as Cawdor snuffed out the light. A second later they were right outside the door. Beside her, Jessie could feel Cawdor picking up the Colt. Then as the men whispered outside the door, Cawdor clicked back the hammer.

Jessie was bringing the .38 from her holster when the door burst open. Cawdor leapt right, firing off a shot as he flew over the bed to the other side. Jessie dove left, rolling on the floor as she fired. A shotgun's blast roared from the door, exploding the feather bed.

Jessie fired again, the bullet slamming into the door as the shotgun lit the room again in a white flash.

Two more shots rang out from Cawdor's gun, then the shotgun-wielding assassins were gone, running down the hall and stairs. A moment later, the front door banged shut. And then another door banged closed.

Jessie and Cawdor took off after them, running down the stairs. When they reached the entranceway, they split up, Jessie going back toward the kitchen, Cawdor continuing on toward the front of the house.

In a matter of seconds, the house was echoing with running feet and shouts.

Seeing nothing, Jessie returned to the front room. Cawdor, too, had come back empty-handed. "Bastards got away," he said.

"You see them? Know their faces?" Jessie asked.

Cawdor shook his head.

"We just have to play it smart now, understand?" Jessie asked.

"Those bastards," Cawdor said. "How could Glamis do this? My father was good to him, damn good. We all were. He was like family."

"Greed," Jessie answered simply.

"Maybe I didn't believe it before, but I sure as hell believe it now," Cawdor hissed. "I truly believe he's behind my father's murder."

"That's good, that's a good start," she answered simply. Jessie could have maybe said something smart. She sure as hell wanted to. But she also knew that Cawdor had to know for himself what kind of man Glamis really was. He had to absorb the facts of his father's murder. He had to let them all sink into his brain so that it made sense for him.

"And I'll tell you what a fine ending's gonna be," Cawdor said, storming away suddenly. "I'm gonna go put a bullet in that son of a bitch's brainpan."

The sudden anger took Jessie by surprise. She had to run to catch up with him, barring his way.

"No, you're not," she said. "You kill him now, they'll hang you."

"Don't care, not at all," Cawdor said. "At least that bastard won't get the place."

"No, he won't," Jessie said. "And you won't, either. Know who will, though?"

The question brought Cawdor up short, stopping him in his tracks as the answer rose quickly in his hate-clouded brain.

Jessie could tell, just by the look on his face, he'd come up with the right answer. "That's right," she said, putting both hands gently on his chest. "Truesday'll get it. Is that what your father would have wanted?"

But just as quickly as the answer to her question had come to him, a solution made itself clear. "Maybe I'll just kill her, too, huh?"

Jessie pushed hard as he started walking forward again. "Go on, you do that," she said. "And how many more? It could get to be a full-time job for you, killing Glamis kin! You could kind of specialize in it."

Jessie's comment struck Cawdor mute. After a moment, she took his hand gently and led him up the stairs. The other guests in the house had settled down, returning to their rooms, no doubt already getting their lies together for the next day.

When they reached Cawdor's room, Jessie guided him inside. He was like a blind man, feeling his way along with great uncertainty.

Jessie smoothed away the feathers, then used a quilt to cover the damage of the shotgun blasts. It would do for the night. There were only a few more hours of darkness left. They could worry about the bed tomorrow.

She had only intended to tuck him back into bed, like a child. But the way he sat there, more than a little confused, on the edge of the bed in his nightshirt, something overtook her. And for the first time, she realized that she was wearing only a flannel nightgown.

When Jessie made to leave, Cawdor reached out, holding her by the shoulders with his strong hands. Kneeling down by his side, she rested her head lightly on his lap. A moment later, he was stroking her blond hair gently.

"It's all gotten very confused," he said. "It's turned bad quickly. Bad like I've never seen it."

"It's okay," Jessie said. "If you're smart about this thing, it will turn out fine."

"I wish it would," he said. "I could lose everything that old man worked a lifetime for. Everything."

She nuzzled into his lap, feeling his firm leg beneath her cheek. "You won't," she answered. "Trust me and Ki, but more importantly, trust yourself. You have to, now."

She stayed like that for a long time. Absentmindedly, she began to stroke his leg with her hand, letting her fingers travel lightly over the worn material of his nightshirt.

Soon, she felt a bulge growing beneath the cloth. It poked her cheek through the material, so that she could feel the warmth coming off it.

Without saying a word, Jessie repositioned herself so that she was kneeling in front of him. Then, very slowly and tentatively, she raised the material of his shirt to reveal the long, swollen shaft.

She studied the shaft for a long time, then, very

71

slowly, she began running her fingers up and down its length, letting just the tips of her fingers barely touch the tightened skin.

When he didn't stop her, she grew bolder, taking the shaft in her hand, feeling the throbbing heat coming off it across her smooth palm. Slowly, slowly, she began to run her hand up and down the shaft.

Cawdor let out a small cry and leaned back on the bed, opening his legs slightly.

Jessie came forward, letting her cheek brush softly against the long shaft, then nuzzling down into the thick thatch of hair. Taking his privates in her hand, she lightly played with them, feeling their weight, as she turned her head to kiss the base of the member.

Cawdor let out a low moan and tried to get up, to ease Jessie into his bed. "No, darling, this is for you," she purred. "Just rest easy."

Slowly then, she began to kiss the thick shaft upward, moving her full, moist lips up its length. When she reached the top, she allowed her tongue to dart out teasingly, softly caressing the smooth skin.

Again and again, she licked around the head of his shaft, until it was glistening in the lamp's dim light. When it shone, she began working her way down, her busy tongue drawing moan after moan from Cawdor.

Soon, the entire length of his shaft was glistening. When she reached the top of his member again, she opened her lips slightly and let the crown slip slowly into her warm, moist mouth. She paused there for a long time, allowing her tongue to slowly, teasingly circle the top. Then, very deliberately, she slid the entire length of his long, hard member into her mouth.

"Oh, Jessie," Cawdor moaned, as he raised his hips up off the bed.

Jessie let the entire length of his shaft rest easily for a long time. Then she began to raise her head, letting the member slip glistening from between her full, pouting lips.

When nearly the whole shaft had escaped her lips, she paused, then lowered herself back down. And again she rested, letting the warm wetness of her mouth caress his manhood for a full minute. Bringing her mouth up slowly, she let the entire length slip from between her lips, then let her hand play along the slick member before taking it into her mouth again.

Soon she was moving her head in a smooth up-and-down rhythm, enjoying the feel of the thick shaft as it filled her, then retreated.

Cawdor moaned again, his hips coming up slowly to meet each of her strokes. She moved faster and faster, then let her hand play along with her lips as she continued to massage his throbbing organ.

Soon he was close to his moment, and Jessie increased her speed, letting her mouth and hand fly up and down his member. A second later, he thrust his hips upward and was filling her as she swallowed greedily.

When he was finished, she paused for a moment, then let her tongue play along the entire length of his shaft, cleaning him in slow smooth caresses.

"Oh, Jessie, that was so—" he began, but Jessie quieted him with a shush.

When she had finished, she lowered the nightshirt and he pulled her up to him, kissing her deeply on the mouth. Lying on top of him, she nuzzled her cheek against his strong chest as he pulled the blanket up around them.

Jessie and Cawdor awoke with a start. Jessie rolled off to find it was morning beyond dawn, and four men stood in the doorway, aiming guns at them.

Reflex brought Jessie's hand over the edge of the bed where the Colt rested.

"Don't even think of it, missy," one of the men said, holding up her gunbelt, " 'cause it ain't there."

"You bastards!" Cawdor shouted. "You low-down thieving sons of bitches!"

"I'd say you're the bastard," one of the men answered.

Jessie, now fully awake, recognized the men as the sheriff and three of his deputies. All of them had taken part in the trap they'd sprung on the rustlers.

"So you're doing Glamis's murdering dirty work for him, is that it?" Cawdor spat, slipping his legs over the side of the bed.

"We're doing the law here, son," the sheriff, a grim-as-death fat man, answered. "Nothing but the law."

"That's what you call what you're doing, law?" Cawdor replied.

"I ain't gonna explain it to you," the sheriff said. "Not like this, anyhow. Now, you get yourself

74

dressed, get this lady dressed, and then we'll talk proper like. But I ain't talking here, not about nothing."

Jessie got up from the bed and one of the deputies followed her to her room. A few minutes later, she returned dressed. Cawdor was dressed, too, the sheriff and two deputies still holding guns on him. "Now, exactly what is it you have to say?" Jessie demanded.

"First off, I want to know where that friend, Ki, got off to," the lawman replied.

"I haven't the slightest idea," Jessie answered. "I haven't seen him since last night."

"No matter. We'll catch him," the sheriff said easily.

"What is it that brings you into this house, this room, holding guns?" Cawdor demanded. "You mind telling me that, sheriff?"

"Wouldn't mind at all," the lawman said, then shifted the gun from one hand to the other, and drew a piece of paper out from his pocket. Flipping open the folded sheet of paper, he said, "This is what brings me here."

Even from across the room, Jessie recognized the sheet of paper as a bill of sale for cattle. She'd seen thousands of them in her life. The scrolling handwriting and printing was as distinctive as printed money. Probably, she'd made up more than a few hundred of them herself. Cawdor's name was signed to the bottom and she recognized that, too. Probably he'd made up more than a couple hundred of them himself with his father's approval.

"It's a bill of sale," Cawdor said.

"You denying it's your writing?" one of the deputies asked.

"Looks like it," Cawdor replied. "Where'd you get it?"

"Now that, son, that's the trick of it," the sheriff answered with a bitter smile. "That there is what's gonna hang you good."

"You're gonna hang me for a bill of sale?" Cawdor asked, incredulously. "In case it's slipped your pea-brain, sheriff, my family's in the cattle business. There's nothing against the law, not in any state, in selling cattle. Hell, I can buy some, if I take a notion to."

"I suppose you can," the lawman answered. "I just reckon you could, if you took yourself a notion to get yourself some cattle, you could."

"That's good," Cawdor replied, speaking as if to a child. "Now whyn't you get yourself and your men out, and go looking for whoever it was that tried to shoot me last night?"

"I could do that," the lawman said, easily. "But right now, I'm gonna take you to jail. Then we're gonna have a little talk about rustling. You, me, and this Starbuck gal. And when we get done talking about rustling, we're gonna set in to talking about how you maybe killed your father. I expect you're gonna have some real original answers for me on that score. Ain't that right?"

In a flash, Cawdor was off the bed, hands out in front of him, ready to choke the life out of the sheriff. But before he could reach the lawman, one of the deputies stepped forward and dealt him a blow with a shotgun butt that sent him sprawling unconscious to the floor.

76

"Now, you got any objections, Miss Starbuck?" the lawman asked.

Jessie didn't answer. She rose from the bed and set about reviving Cawdor.

★

Chapter 8

The lawman explained it to Jessie and Cawdor only when the two were locked in separate cells in the jail. The way the story went was that one of the men from the posse had "come into possession" of the dead rustler's boots. The boots were so worn and shabby, not to mention a pinch too tight, that the ranch hand had decided to cut off the tops for bullet pouches.

"Well, you can just imagine his shock when he came across this bill of sale," the sheriff said, relishing the story. "It explains just about everything.",

"It doesn't explain anything," Cawdor protested. "It doesn't explain one damn thing. Not as far as I'm concerned."

The lawman smiled, stepping close to the prison cell's bars. "See, that's just exactly where you're wrong," he said. "It tells me how a bunch of raggedy-ass rustlers could make off with cattle from your daddy's ranch and have no trouble selling them across the border. Tells me that you were more than just maybe in on the whole deal from the start. Tells me that maybe you were in it to steal from others, too. That's what it tells me."

Jessie saw the way it was immediately. Glamis had failed to kill them the night before, but by morning he'd hatched a new plan. And it was a good one, she had to give him that. Now, the only question remaining was how long the trial would take. No doubt, Glamis had thought of that, too.

"What are we gonna do, Jessie?" Cawdor asked when the sheriff strode back out to the front office, closing the door after him.

"Judge is set to pass through again soon, isn't he?" Jessie asked.

"Couple of weeks," Cawdor said. "But hell, we can't spend a couple weeks locked up. Not with Glamis running the ranch."

"If I could maybe get a message out," Jessie said. "I could do something. Contact the governor."

"What do you mean 'if'?" Cawdor snapped. "Let's do that exact thing. Let's do it now."

Jessie sat down on the bunk, thinking. Glamis wasn't about to wait a few weeks for the circuit judge to ride through. She'd seen his kind before. He wasn't the type to throw the dice with a fair trial. The way she saw it, Glamis would pull the same stunt he had with the rustler. The obituary would read, "Killed while escaping." Rising back up off the bunk, she approached the bars closest to Cawdor's cell. "I need you to listen to me," she said. "I need you to listen real close."

"About that message, right?"

"There won't be a message," Jessie said. "I could

write from now to forever and they'd never get it to the governor."

The young man seemed to visibly slump down into himself when the knowledge of what they were up against sank into his brain. "What shall we do then?"

Jessie began pacing. "I'll tell you what we're *not* going to do," she said. "We're not going to try to escape. Let them leave the door open, let them get careless, but we're not going to make a move. You understand that? Because the second we do, I promise you, they'll shoot us down like dogs. Do it in the street, just to have witnesses. You understand?"

"I understand," Cawdor answered. "So we'll just sit here and wait, is that it?"

The days passed slowly. Just like Jessie had said, the men guarding them began to get careless after the first day. They entered the cells, guns strapped on, and turned their backs on the prisoners as much as they could. Twice, during the first week, they left the door to the cells open. Once, they left the keys within easy reach.

Jessie knew that Glamis and his men could kill them at any time, but they wanted to do it in public. Gunning down the son of a rancher would raise more than a few eyebrows in a town hungry for gossip and scandal. It didn't particularly matter on whose side the scandal fell, just as long as folks had something to shake their heads at and cluck over. And Glamis was smart in that way. He wanted to keep all the scandal on his side. It had to be done out in the open, so nobody would be left doubting.

After six days had passed, they started cutting back on the food. No doubt, the men were trying to starve Jessie and Cawdor out. Jessie wasn't having any of it. But Cawdor was a different matter. He was getting madder by the day. Jessie could see the desperation in his eyes. Maybe it was because he was locked up for a crime he didn't commit, but more than likely, it was knowing that Glamis, the man who'd killed his father, was now walking free. Not only was he walking free, but living in a house and eating the food that was due Cawdor.

Jessie didn't know how much longer she could keep Cawdor calm enough not to try and escape. She hoped he could last another week, until the judge came. That's what she hoped, but she was wrong.

Cawdor made his move after supper on the seventh day. The guard came in to collect the plates and the young man jumped him.

"Cawdor, no!" Jessie roared. But it was too late. Cawdor had the guard down and the gun out of the holster before Jessie could cross the small distance of her cell.

"I don't care," Cawdor screamed back, laying the guard out with a sharp blow to the head. "I can't take it. I won't take it. That lying, thieving bastard, he's going to die. One way or another, I'm going to get that bastard for what he's done!"

"Walk out that door and you're a dead man," Jessie warned. "That's just what he and his men are waiting for."

"I stay here and I'm a dead man," Cawdor answered. "Now, are you with me or no?"

Jessie nodded slowly, and in a moment, Cawdor had the ring of keys off the wall peg and was unlocking her cell. They had one gun between them. Beyond the door, in the sheriff's office, was a rack of shotguns and rifles. And beyond that, the street.

Cawdor was halfway to the door when Jessie pulled him back. "You don't think they're going to let you walk on out, do you?"

"That's a chance I got to take," the young man said.

"Well, then, let's just shift the odds a little our way," Jessie said and pulled him toward the back door.

Cawdor led the way, gun out in front of him. Slowly opening the door, he moved through cautiously.

An instant later, an ax handle crashed against his stomach, doubling him over. Jessie jumped, grabbing the length of ash firmly, and startling the guard so badly he released it. A sharp jab with the end to the guard's privates sent him to the ground as Jessie helped Cawdor up and retrieved the gun.

"Can you run?" Jessie asked.

Cawdor nodded, still winded, and they made off across the vacant lot.

Two shots rang out from the injured guard and Cawdor turned and squeezed down on the trigger. The hammer clicked down, misfiring on the round. He pulled back again, and again the gun didn't fire. "Son of a bitch, they set us up," Cawdor screamed, throwing the gun down.

"That some kind of surprise to you?" Jessie asked, as the first shots kicked up dirt at their feet.

Half a minute later, they were running through back lots, scaring chickens and women hanging laundry. It couldn't have gone better for Glamis if they'd helped him plan it. All around they could hear men shouting as the chase continued.

Turning, Jessie saw three men in pursuit. Two of them had repeaters, the third a shotgun. As they approached an alley, one of the men with a repeater stopped and began firing. Wood on the corner building began chipping away at throat level.

Jessie's boots struggled for purchase on the dry ground as she turned the corner, Cawdor just in front of her. Ahead, she heard more shouts and the sounds of boots running on the boards of the main street.

Four men, all with shotguns, rounded the corner in front of them, bringing Jessie and Cawdor to a stop. Cawdor began raising his hands, hoping that maybe that would do some good. Jessie stepped over to the other side of the alley. The alley was narrow, maybe five feet across. Blind men could hit them with shotguns.

It was then that Jessie saw the wagon. It was a ranch wagon with a two-horse team and a young brunette up on the front seat.

"What you boys all doing?" she asked.

The men stopped and turned. One of them began to say something, but then the girl reached down and came up with a Wells Fargo ten-gauge. "Got this here gun loaded with twenty dimes, each barrel," she purred sweetly. "You reckon I could hit something from here?"

Jessie figured she could hit all of them from the mouth of the alley. Jessie couldn't see the men's faces, but she would bet they were surprised. All of them dropped the scatterguns.

And Jessie wasted no time. She ran forward, just

as Ki popped his head up from the side of the wagon. He wasn't smiling as Jessie and Cawdor approached. Then his hand flashed and Jessie saw a glint and felt the throwing star whisper past her eye. A moment later one of the gunmen behind her was shouting in pain.

"I'm much obliged," Cawdor said as he and Jessie clambered up the wagon's side. The wagon was already moving by the time they had hold of the sides.

A moment later, they were galloping out of town, bullets singing in the air around their heads and gouging into the wagon as the horses charged ahead.

"This is Rosalie," Ki said, as the bullets and shouts faded in the distance.

"Rosalie, what in hell are you doing here?" Cawdor asked, annoyed.

"I just quit," she said. "Can't take that Truesday no more. That woman, she ain't—well—she just ain't normal!"

"And you just figured on getting yourself a wagon and a ten-gauge?" Cawdor persisted.

"I'd say that just now, well, you ain't in no position to question me," she said breathlessly, slapping down hard on the reins. In a few minutes they'd have riders out. "But no, I came to town and met up with Mr. Ki here. And he seemed to have a plan and I didn't have none. And, well, it all worked out."

"They're coming," Jessie said, turning around to see a half dozen horsemen on the trail behind them.

"How far is the river from this spot?" Ki asked, looking out over the fields on both sides.

"Half mile, across that way," Cawdor answered.

"The cave!" Jessie cried suddenly, and saw the flash of recognition in Cawdor's face.

"Turn off, Rosalie, now!" Cawdor cried.

The young woman struggled, bringing the horses off the road and into one of the fields. In a moment they were galloping through tall grass. "What about this cave?" she asked.

"We used to play there when we were young," Jessie said. "You ever tell anyone about it, Cawdor?"

"Haven't been there in years," he answered.

Behind them, the horsemen were gaining. And ahead was the river.

When they reached the tree line, all four abandoned the wagon and ran for the river, plunging down the muddy bank into the icy water. They moved quickly, running shin deep over the smooth stones. A quarter mile down, the water deepened. The opposite bank was a straight, stony slope.

"There! I remember that tree!" Jessie said and plunged into the water, swimming across the current.

The others followed. When they reached the other side, Jessie dove and vanished beneath the overhang. Cawdor followed, then Rosalie, and finally Ki.

They came up in a cavern the size of a small shack, illuminated like twilight by several small openings at the top. The water was waist high. A dry, narrow ledge ran along one wall, forming a natural bench.

"We can wait them out here," Jessie said, panting.

The others nodded, solemnly. There would be some

planning to do, but right now, they were content to wait and listen as they heard the posse shouting above them.

Rosalie broke the silence, saying, "Well don't this just remind me of a Fort Worth hotel."

"Jessie and I would come here when we were young," Cawdor said. "I haven't thought about this place for years."

"Ki, how did you know?" Jessie asked. "How'd you know we'd try to escape?"

"I did not know," he answered. "Not for certain. But I had the horses ready, and the wagon. I did know that you could not continue in prison. I suspect they would have shot you in a cell, if they could not shoot you escaping."

"How come they didn't arrest you?" Cawdor asked.

"They could not," Ki said. "Rosalie provided my alibi. I remained in town as a witness. Twice I sent telegraphs to the governor. And twice they were not received or not sent. There was an unfortunate incident in the hotel and another at the telegraph office. Glamis's men. I decided to stay in town as a witness."

"What's going on back there?" Jessie asked. "They all went crazy."

"It's Glamis," Rosalie put in. "He's throwing money around town like it ain't his—"

"It's not," Cawdor said quickly. "It's not his damn money. It's mine."

Rosalie gave him a look of apology and continued. "He's bought the sheriff and all the deputies," she added. "Buying supplies he don't need and every other thing you can think. Cawdor, I'm sorry to

86

say, you just ain't got no more friends in this town. Whatever people you called your friends, Glamis went and bought them. They came cheap, too. Some of them, all it took was a bottle of whiskey or a three-dollar woman."

"What're we gonna do, Jessie?" Cawdor asked, his voice a low rumble of true despair.

"Wait till dark, then start out," she said, as all faces turned in her direction. "That's the only chance we have now, traveling at night."

"Start out where?" Rosalie asked. "Where we gonna start out to?"

"I didn't see Delgado at the funeral," Jessie said. "Is the old man still alive? He didn't sell out, did he?"

"The old man had a stroke," Cawdor answered, "can't get around. Runs his ranch from a bed and a wheelchair from what I hear. Haven't been out there in years, but folks say that it's truly something to see. He has a kind of a table fixed up for himself. Big window put in with a brass telescope like they use on ships. Sees the spread better than when he was riding. Got a daughter, Miranda, who helps."

"Who's Delgado?" Rosalie asked. "I can't say that I ever heard of him."

"Rancher, about twenty, twenty-five miles down the river," Jessie said. "Got a nice little spread. Your father ended on good terms with him, did he?"

"Sure," Cawdor answered. "But I don't know if he'll help. Maybe horses, I don't know."

"It's worth a chance," Jessie said. "I don't see anyplace else to go."

"You know, almost went to Chicago once," Rosalie said. "Almost went to work for this

87

banker. You think I made the wrong choice, Ki?"

"The choice is either work for banker or hide in a cave, wet, and a fugitive?" he asked.

"Yes, I guess that's it," she said. "Live in a big house with marble floors and a fireplace in every room. Nice little uniform, cleaned twice a week. Hot baths."

"How in hell could you ask that?" Cawdor said. "Of course you made the right choice. What in hell kind of life is that for a young lady, working for a banker? And in Chicago! It's not—"

"Moral?" Ki suggested.

"Exactly," Cawdor agreed. "And a Chicago banker! Rosalie, I'm shocked and dismayed. Truly. And if they don't hang us, we're gonna have to have ourselves a little talk."

★

Chapter 9

They waited until it was completely dark before emerging, wet and cold, from the cave. It would be a long walk and a long night. And they would have to walk the distance in water, just in case the posse had hounds positioned along the river.

Progress was slow. They walked until well after dawn before taking their first rest, and then, only for a few minutes' time. It was past noon when the river opened up to a wide bend, both sides flanked by lush fields of grazing land.

"What do you figure, another few miles?" Cawdor asked.

"About that," Jessie answered.

Turning the bend, they heard the first shot. It was no more than a dim echo, but it was enough to stop them in their watery tracks.

"Is someone shooting at us?" Rosalie asked, crouching low.

The next shot answered her question, when a

fist-size chunk of bark exploded at head-level from a tree on the far bank.

Cawdor went for his gun, but Jessie shouted, "No," freezing his hand midway to the pistol's butt. She knew it was senseless to start shooting.

"Who are you going to shoot?" Jessie asked. It was a good question. All around, they saw no one in sight. Only a dim puff of powder smoke drifted off in the distance.

"I would suggest we raise our hands," Ki offered, then demonstrated.

Jessie followed Ki's example, then Cawdor, and finally Rosalie. When all four had their hands raised, they stood there studying the landscape. Still, nobody appeared.

"That's good, that's the way to do it," a voice cried from the pasture. "Now, you all just walk toward me. Do it nice and slow. One twitch and I'd feel obliged to blow your heads off, one at a time."

Hands still raised, the four began to cross toward the pasture, moving easily between the few cows who had lowered their heads to drink. As the four moved up on dry land, the cows barely offered them a curious look.

"We're looking for the Delgado spread," Jessie called.

"We're friends," Cawdor added.

"Well, you picked one helluva way to come calling," the voice said. "Most friends come around the front way. Now, throw down them guns."

Cawdor went for the side arm, but the voice stopped him. "Real easy like," the voice advised. "Pull it out real slow."

Cawdor and Jessie threw their guns down in front of them.

Unbeknownst to any of them, Ki had secreted a throwing star between the fingers of his left hand. It would take him no more than a blink of an eye to bring it into position and send it sailing toward its target—that is, if the target would be courteous enough to show himself.

When Jessie began to lower her hands, the voice said, "Keep them up there, little lady. Just keep waving them fingers in the breeze."

"Who are you?" Cawdor shouted.

"You work for Delgado?" Jessie added.

It was then that the gunman showed himself for the first time. He rose not a hundred yards directly in front of them, coming up out of the ground like a rabbit. A Sharps .50 long rifle was held firmly against his shoulder. "Right now, I'd judge none of you to be in any kind of position to ask questions," the man said. "Now, all of you, turn 'round."

They did as they were told, showing the gunman their backs. A moment later, three rapid shots rang out from his revolver. In the distance, three answered.

It took nearly half an hour, but they arrived. Jessie could hear them coming, the horses trotting behind her over the open field.

"Let's see what we got here, then," another voice said. "Whyn't you folks just turn 'round."

They did, and there, sitting tall in the saddle, was Delgado's daughter, Miranda. She was black-haired and lovely. In fact, when both were young girls, people had called Miranda a darker version of Jessie.

"Lower those guns, boys. I know these hardcases," Miranda said, smiling.

An hour later they were sitting in the drawing room of the Delgado house, a large adobe structure that enclosed a small stone courtyard. The old man had come across the river from Mexico as a young man and had never gone back. But he'd built a house that looked for all the world a replica of the grand haciendas of the wealthy Mexican land owners.

"I got to tell you, that's one helluva story," Miranda said, sitting back in a large leather chair. "Just one helluva story."

"What about those men?" Rosalie asked. "Do you always plant gunmen in the field?"

Miranda laughed at this. "Never thought to put it like that," she said. "Thinking on it, I suppose I'd be afraid of what would grow from them. No, they're for the rustlers. Probably should call 'em off, after what you folks told me."

"Can you help us?" Jessie asked, leaning forward eagerly.

The dark-haired woman studied Jessie for a long time, her eyes searching for the trace of a lie or deception. "Can't think of what we could do," she said at last. "Damn, I can help you get across the border, but that wouldn't solve nothing. Let's just think on it and see what we come up with."

"Miranda, how's your father doing?" Cawdor asked. "I haven't seen him for a spell."

"Cranky as always," she said. "Planting those boys out by the river was his idea, though I expect it wasn't a bad one. Just silly. Made them feel silly, hiding in the ground like rabbits. But it worked, on you folks, anyway. Come on, I'll take you up to visit."

"We don't want to disturb him," Jessie offered.

"Disturb him? Hell, he'll welcome the company," came the young woman's answer.

The stairway up to the second floor was lined with an array of ropes, cables and pulleys stretched tight against the wall. It resembled a ship's deck, with complicated pulley arrangements at the top and bottom.

"Something he's working on. Contraption to get him up and down the stairs in the wheelchair," Miranda explained. "Might just work if he ever figures it out all the way and we can talk one of the hands into testing it out."

"He could move his bed downstairs," Cawdor suggested. "It might be a bit easier on him and the hand."

"No, he's fine up there. Likes it up there," she answered. "Just a matter of making that contraption work, is all."

The five of them climbed the stairs to the second floor. At the end of the hall, a large wooden door, heavy enough for a church, stood closed. Miranda stepped up to the iron reinforced door and knocked. She knocked lightly, so lightly that Jessie suspected that it might just be impossible to hear such a knock from the inside.

But Delgado heard the knock. From inside the room a voice shouted, "Bring 'em in, dammit!"

Miranda opened the door and the small parade marched respectfully into the bedroom. It was actually more an office than a bedroom. The bed was obscured by a screen, a large desk, covered with papers, stood along one wall, and a smaller writing desk was arranged against another wall. Newly built double windows led out to a small balcony that boasted a long brass telescope mounted on the forward facing railing.

The old man was out on the balcony, sitting in a wheelchair, facing the pasture. As soon as the five of them were in the room, he wheeled the ancient wood and wicker chair around to face his guests.

Delgado was the same man that Jessie remembered from her youth. He had a dark, strong-featured face, but his hair, once black as coal, was now silvered with gray. Indeed, age had taken its toll on every feature except the eyes. The eyes still burned with a passion. And then, of course, he was sitting in the chair, both feet turned just slightly in. He was dressed the same as Jessie remembered him, too—the same as he always dressed—in a black suit and white shirt.

"Well, Jessica Starbuck," Delgado said. "Step forward and give me a kiss."

Jessie came forward and bent to embrace the old man. "It's good to see you," she whispered, as she rose.

"Damn, but you grew up," Delgado answered. "And that's Ki there, ain't it?"

Ki came forward to shake hands with the old man and offer a small smile.

"What else we got here?" the old man asked. "Cawdor Birnam, I believe."

Cawdor came forward to shake hands, and knowing that the old man had no way of recognizing Rosalie, he made the introduction.

"Well, I saw it all," Delgado said. "Saw you folks tramping down the river. Now, I'd say all of you are just a touch too old to be hunting frogs, so I'm waiting to hear the story."

"First off, Poppa, we can bring the men in," Miranda said. "That problem we had was taken care of, upriver."

"That's good, then," the old man said, wheeling himself forward. "Can't say I care for my men hiding in holes. Not with work to be done."

"Also, they have a problem," Miranda added.

"Of course they have a problem," the old man snapped back. "Walking around in the river, coming in like drowned rats. Any blind man, which I ain't, could see that. Now, let's just have them tell it to us."

And they did tell it. First Jessie, then Cawdor. With each new segment of the story, the old man's face twisted down into more of a frown. By the time the story ended, he was frowning hard, but thinking, too.

"What about the law?" Delgado asked.

"Sheriff's bought and paid for," Cawdor said. "Deputies are too, I'd say."

"The sheriff," Delgado spat, as if cursing. "No, I meant the real law. Rangers, son. What did the Rangers have to say on the matter?"

"We haven't seen them," Cawdor said.

"Well, son, that's your problem," the old man said. "That there is your problem, pure and simple."

"Nearest one's a three-day ride," Jessie added.

"Not from here, he ain't," Delgado corrected.

Cawdor and Jessie looked at each other.

"Miranda, you go down and pull one of those old boys out of a hole and give him a horse," the old man ordered. "Have him ride out directly. Tell him not to come back unless he's riding next to a Ranger."

"Now?" she asked.

"Damn right now," Delgado said. "None of us here are getting any younger, least of all me."

"What do we do in the meanwhile?" Cawdor asked.

Delgado studied all of them for a long time before answering. "Now, I'd just be guessing here," he said, "but I'd say you folks didn't sleep last night and didn't eat this morning. What with jail-breaking and all. Now, what I'm telling you to do, directly, is have that worthless cook kill a couple of chickens. Then, I'm sending you all to bed."

Miranda led them from the room and back down the stairs.

"He's still a scrapper, isn't he?" Cawdor asked, when they were far from the thick door.

"Still thinks he is," Miranda said. "He's slowing down some and he's mad as hell about it. That stroke didn't help his disposition any, either."

Fed and put to bed, Jessie found herself facing Cawdor beneath a patchwork quilt. The feather bed on which they rested felt good. Naked, she huddled close to the young man as the day's last light broke in through the shuttered window.

"Do you think it will work?" she asked. "Calling in the Rangers?"

"Yes, of course. They can't be bought," he answered. Then he reached out and gently, his hand began to caress her breast.

Jessie moved in closer. "It's turned into a mess. I'm sorry, really."

"And I'm sorry you got dragged into it," he said, his finger tracing the smooth, silky perfection of her

96

breast, beginning with the underside then circling up slowly until he was lightly teasing her nipple.

Jessie reached her own hand out and placed it on his firm hip. He came in closer and she felt the electric charge of desire pass between them.

Taking her pert nipple between two fingers, he rolled it slowly, feeling it harden under his touch. When it was fully erect, he continued to tease it, circling it with just the very tip of one finger, until moving on to the other.

Jessie let out a low moan, then let her hand slide down between his legs. His shaft was already hard or nearly so. Using just two fingers, she teased the underside, drawing a moan from the young man.

Cawdor abandoned her breasts and sent his hand sliding down her smooth, firm belly, then over her inner thigh, lightly stroking the smooth flesh with the gentlest touch Jessie could imagine.

She rolled over slowly, resting on her back, and parted her legs. Cawdor's hand moved up her thigh, brushed against her silken thatch, then retraced its journey.

Jessie, taking his shaft in her hand, began to massage him fully, using long, sensuous strokes.

Cawdor continued to tease her, running his fingers up and down her long thighs, each time lingering just a little longer at her moist womanhood. And each time, doing something just a little different.

When she could stand it no longer, she pulled herself up on to him, guiding his shaft effortlessly into her in one long movement.

They stayed completely motionless for a long time. Then Cawdor reached up and, cupping her breasts in both hands, let his thumbs stray up teasingly over her nipples. The tingling sensation sent Jessie squirming as the shaft slid halfway out of her.

Soon she was rolling her hips in long rotations as she lifted herself up and then down again on the member. Cawdor, now accustomed to her lovemaking, matched every stroke, knowing just what to do to draw the small sighs of pleasure from her.

As their lovemaking grew faster, she threw her head back and closed her eyes. Cawdor looked up, seeing her bathed in the ruby light of a Texas sunset. It was, he suspected, the most beautiful thing he'd ever see. The image engraved itself in his brain and he knew, even as an old man, he'd be able to recall the scene vividly with a warm flush of pleasure.

Jessie reached her moment, bringing her hands up from his strong thighs to hold him firmly by the shoulders as she shuddered again and again in pleasure. A moment later, she could feel Cawdor spending himself within her, warming her with renewed pleasure.

A short time later, he held her from behind as they lay like spoons together in the deep down bed. His strong arms encircled her own and one gentle hand cupped her breast.

Jessie wiggled slightly, arranging herself into him, feeling the warmth of his organ against her skin. "I'm sure it will be fine, everything will be fine," she crooned, closing her eyes as sleep claimed her.

"I hope so, Jessie," Cawdor whispered back. "I know a lot of men—good men—died over that land. I'd just hate like hell to have a bastard like Glamis end up with it."

Jessie hugged him closer in response. She knew

that somewhere out there, in the fading sun, one of Delgado's men was riding fast, anxious to reach the Rangers. If they were lucky, he'd find them by tomorrow. At most it would be two, maybe three days, and then they could return to Cawdor's ranch and set things right.

In a bedroom down the hall, Cawdor heard a small moan and knew that Ki and Rosalie were making love. He wondered if they were having as much pleasure as he and Jessie had just had. Jessie was one helluva woman; no other words came to his mind to describe her. She had always been a real hellfire, ever since they were both knee-high to grasshoppers.

Cawdor promised himself that when this was all over, he'd tell her what he really thought of her. Just come out and say it.

Suddenly, Cawdor realized that one way or another, everything would turn out for the best. He knew for a fact that he could depend on Jessie and Ki. They were more like family—a long-lost family perhaps—than friends. And when the game got rough, there was no one he could think of that he'd rather have watching his back. And he counted on Delgado and his men to come through for him. At the very least, he knew that Miranda would not give them away to the Rangers or the local sheriff.

But in the end, it would be up to him. It was his land by right and birth. And when all was said and done, he was the only one who could reclaim it. He would have to take it back for himself. That was the way it was and the way it always had been.

★
Chapter 10

They woke early the next day to a big Texas
breakfast. All of them, even Miranda, ate with a
sense of expectancy, as if they might be interrupted
at any moment. But help never comes fast enough,
while trouble just comes too quickly.

They had to wait until lunch for the Ranger to
arrive. It was the old man who spotted them first,
the hand and the ranger, riding hard from the south.
He spotted them with his telescope on the balcony
and called down, announcing their arrival.

By the time the Ranger rode up, they were all
gathered at the front of the house to greet him.

He was a big man who rode a fine looking claybank
with a California saddle and a Winchester repeater
in a boot. He stepped down off the horse with a
serious ease, dutifully tipped his hat to the ladies,
and shook hands with the men. He said his name
was Adam Gathers. "As in Adam Gathers, Eve eats,"
he said, making a small, worn joke.

Jessie and Cawdor told him their story, which

by now was becoming just as worn, over a pot of coffee.

Gathers nodded thoughtfully, his slate-gray eyes searching out the smallest lie.

When they were done talking, Jessie and Cawdor sat back to see just what the Ranger would say. "Seems we got one hell of a problem," he said, taking a final sip of his black coffee. "But maybe it ain't the one you want to know about."

"And what would that be?" Jessie asked.

"Well, two problems, really," Gathers said. "First one is you and Cawdor are wanted outlaws. That's in the eyes of the law, in my eyes. Second one is, if you're telling the truth, it's gonna be damned hard to prove."

"Does that mean you're going to arrest us?" Rosalie asked, her voice full of concern.

Somehow Jessie didn't think the Ranger would arrest them. If he was going to take them all back for trial, then he'd have said so before.

"No, not just yet," Gathers answered. "Don't have enough to arrest you for, yet. But that don't mean I can let you all walk around free. That wouldn't be right, either."

"What do you suggest then?" Cawdor asked.

Gathers rubbed his strong chin thoughtfully. When that didn't produce an idea, he combed his fingers through the length of light brown hair on his head. He seemed to have better luck with his hair and kept doing it for some time, until an idea formed under it. "Here's what we're going to do," he said finally. "Miss Starbuck, you and Mr. Birnam are coming back with me. Rosalie and Ki, if I have your word that you two won't try to escape, then I

101

can leave you on here, as house prisoners."

"That sounds, just—" Cawdor began to say.

"I wasn't asking your permission," Gathers cut him off quickly. "What I'm saying is, that's the way it's going to be, exactly. If it don't suit you, then I'm a little sorry, but not much."

"What's your plan, just ride into town and ask the sheriff?" Jessie asked. She couldn't keep the sarcasm out of her voice. She knew that the odds were stacked against them. As it stood now, it was their word against Glamis's. And they were, after everything was said and done, escaped prisoners.

"Something like that," Gathers replied, fixing her in his steely gaze. "But I figured we'd pay a call on the ranch. Just to see what those folks are up to. That is, if that suits you, Miss Starbuck?"

"Not much," Jessie replied, but she let it drop at that. She had nothing but the highest respect for Rangers, but in this particular case, with her neck on the line, she was beginning to have her doubts.

"Okay then, it's agreed," Gathers said. "We can ride out tomorrow at first light."

They set out the next day just after dawn. Jessie was grateful that Gathers had let her and Cawdor keep their guns, though there was little danger of them shooting him in the back, since he rode along three or four paces behind their horses. It was never stated that he mistrusted them, yet to ride in such a way showed a suspicion. Jessie really couldn't blame him. The suspicious, she knew, tended to live longer. Sometimes they lived quite a bit after the trusting souls had been buried and forgotten.

It was a two-day ride to the Birnam spread, and

by the end of the first day, they made camp by a small stand of trees. Jessie had spent the hour before wondering if Gathers would take their guns when they bedded down for the night. Her question was answered when he spread out his bedroll far from the fire, on the other side of the horses. If they were going to shoot him in his sleep, it would be a tricky shot indeed. The very second they approached Gathers, the horses would have woken him from his sleep.

Halfway through the second day, the Ranger moved his horse up closer, nearly between Jessie and Cawdor.

"Seems to me I heard that name, Glamis, before," he said casually.

"On a dodger, I'd bet," Cawdor said.

Gathers shook his head. "Not quite," he said. "Something though. Heard it from a rustler up north a bit. Then again, heard something about a husband and wife team working saloons with a crooked game. Nothing to go on. Seem to remember they came from Philadelphia, leastways, that's where they said they were from."

"Damn, that's what he told us! Told my pa," Cawdor said. "Told him he was a preacher's boy."

"That sounds familiar, too," Gathers answered. "Something about being orphaned."

"That's it, that's your man!" Cawdor nearly whooped. "Both parents dead of yellow fever. Came west with his wife. Let's go lock that bastard up, directly!"

"Hold on there now," Gathers cautioned. "I didn't say he was wanted for nothing. I just said I knew the name, can't remember where from or the particulars.

Could be he built a school for crippled orphans and homes for fat widows. Could have read about him in a magazine."

"He's not from a magazine, Gathers," Cawdor said, getting mad now. "He's straight from hell."

"Hold on and I'll tell you what I will do," Gathers said in a consoling voice. "I'll send word back and find out what there is to find out. That suit you?"

"Not as much as a hanging would," Cawdor mumbled, and spurred his horse on a little faster.

"That boy, he's got a temper," Gathers said to Jessie. "If he don't keep it reined in tight, it's going to land him in some genuine trouble."

"Hell, he's lost his father, the ranch, and he's wanted for murder," Jessie replied. "Just what is your idea of genuine trouble, Mr. Gathers?"

The Ranger allowed himself a small smile and turned toward Jessie. "Having me on your trail," he stated simply. "Not to brag on myself, but I'd say that's about the worst possible kind of trouble anyone could ask for."

Jessie didn't doubt, and she didn't answer. She knew Gathers wasn't bragging. She also knew that what he was saying was a warning to her. It was a warning that told her to not try to escape and to keep Cawdor from trying as well.

They reached the property line at noon. They rode the fence for an hour before spotting the house. A small chill ran up Jessie's spine in the midday heat. Everything was going to be decided in the next few hours.

As they came closer to the house, Jessie saw that it bore little resemblance to the place she'd left just a few days before. A dozen men were setting about painting it. The new coat of white paint seemed odd in such country, where most folks let the sun and rain take its toll. But the thing that really struck her was that the house resembled nothing so much as an armed encampment. Everywhere there were men with guns. They loafed around the back and on the roof. Two men with rifles sat on the rail fence of the corral.

Jessie gave Cawdor a sideways glance and saw that his eyes were open wide. Glamis had turned the place into a fort.

"Looks to me like they're expecting someone," Gathers said, himself a little shaken by the sight.

A few of the men brought their guns up as the trio approached. Immediately, Jessie raised her hands, as did Cawdor and Gathers.

A dozen of the men abandoned their positions, meeting them in the pasture as they rode in. A dozen rifles and pistols pointed at the three riders. Jessie recognized some of the faces as those from the posse. They were the sheriff's deputies.

"Ranger," Gathers said. "Here to see a fella named Glamis."

The men didn't answer and they didn't lower their guns, even with Gathers's announcement or sight of the Ranger badge he wore on his chest. All of them, an even dozen, stood there openmouthed and silent. Then one of the men shouted, "Boss! Boss!"

Everyone stayed frozen for a full minute, before a figure emerged from the back of the house. Even from a hundred and fifty yards off, Jessie recognized the man as Glamis.

The figure came down off the stairs and walked

slowly toward the gathering. When he was close enough to recognize faces, he hesitated, but just for a second.

The hatred welling up inside him, Cawdor made a move, a sudden jerking action toward his gun. A half-dozen hammers came back, poised over shells, and the sound of three or four rifles jacking shells into their chambers broke the air.

"Steady there, son," Gathers said, not turning to look at Cawdor. He didn't have to; he could see where all the guns were pointed.

When Glamis was close enough, he walked casually through the circle of gunmen and studied the three riders.

"You Glamis?" Gathers asked.

"That's me," came the slow answer. "Now who in hell are you?"

"Name's Gathers," the Ranger said. "Texas Ranger. You know these folks?"

Glamis ignored the question. "That's what that badge says, Texas Ranger. How am I supposed to know that's who you are?"

" 'Cause I just told you," Gathers answered, annoyed.

"Could be some gunslick the little bastard hired to put a bullet in me," Glamis mused. "If I shot you now, nobody would blame me."

"Nobody but the Rangers," Gathers answered. "They'd blame you and hang you. These men, they might get off easy, twenty-five years apiece."

A couple of the gunmen wavered, but not much. Apparently they were more afraid of Glamis than twenty-five years in a prison.

"If you are who you say, a Ranger, how come these

people, these killers, still got their guns?" Glamis asked.

The question was met by a general mumbling of agreement by the men surrounding them.

" 'Cause I let them keep 'em," Gathers answered. "No other reason."

Then Jessie saw another figure appear at the door. It was a woman, Truesday no doubt. She was wearing a blue dress that shimmered in the heat. On her head was a large hat with an ornate feather.

"Now I got papers in my pocket that I'm gonna reach out," Gathers said. "Papers that say I'm a Ranger."

"You reach for them, nice and slow like," Glamis said.

Gathers, moving cautiously, brought out a small cowhide wallet. He tossed the wallet to Glamis, who caught it easily. Opening the wallet, he extracted the papers and read them, moving his lips slightly.

"I'm putting my hands down now," Gathers said, lowering his hands.

Jessie and Cawdor followed suit.

"Not them!" Glamis ordered. "Maybe you are a Ranger, but these folks, they're murdering scum."

"That's what I'm here to find out," Gathers said.

"That's what you're here to find out, is it?" Glamis answered. "Well, I figure I can tell you what you need to know to put a rope around their necks. Now come down, nice and slow."

Gathers, squinting with rage, did as he was told. He was not a man accustomed to taking orders and didn't like the idea of being given them now. Even if this Glamis jasper were being careful, he was disrespecting the badge of the Texas Rangers and that was something Gathers could not stomach. Not for an instant.

When Gathers was down off the saddle, Glamis turned his attention to Jessie and Cawdor. "You, too, both of you come down, nice and easy. And somebody take those damn guns away."

When the men had the guns secured in the front of their pants, Glamis said, "Bring them near the house. Line 'em up against the fence. And somebody take their damn horses in the pen while I talk to this so-called Ranger."

Jessie and Cawdor watched from the fence as Glamis led Gathers inside the house.

"You boys are making a big mistake here," Cawdor said, addressing the four men who now watched them. "That Ranger wasn't lying when he said twenty-five years."

"Shut up!" one of the men said. "We'll just wait and see what happens now, won't we?"

They didn't have to wait long. No more than a minute passed before a gunshot boomed from inside the house. A second later, Glamis came smashing through a window, the glass shattering loudly as he fell.

They all watched as Gathers followed Glamis out the window, though more gracefully. The Ranger landed on his feet, picked Glamis up, and punched powerfully at his head. Somehow he'd lost his gun inside the house. All he had was his fists, but they seemed to be enough.

Two of the men guarding Jessie and Cawdor ran to help their boss as Gathers propped Glamis against the house and sent a fist plunging into the man's gut.

Jessie didn't hesitate. Kicking out, she sank the toe of her boot into a gunman's groin, then leapt forward, grabbing his rifle by the barrel to aim it up, over her shoulder. An instant later a shot sounded, frightening the horses in the corral.

Cawdor, too, had sprung into action, reaching out for the other guard's gun hand with one hand as he sent a hard punch into the man's face with the other. Twisting hard, he managed to relieve the guard of the gun, just as Jessie raised the butt of the rifle and smashed it across the other guard's head.

When Jessie and Cawdor looked again, they saw Gathers, bleeding from the lip and nose, standing over Glamis, who lay panting on the ground.

Jessie felt the beginning of a smile form on her face, but an instant later it was frozen in shock. Around the corner, dressed up like a banker's wife, Truesday advanced on Gathers, a scattergun in her hands.

"Behind you!" Jessie yelled.

Gathers turned, fists already up as Truesday pulled both triggers. The double-blast propelled Gathers backward, splattering the freshly painted wall and nearly cutting him in half in the process.

Suddenly, from all around, shots were ringing out. Her face contorted into a murderous mask, Truesday broke open the gun and fished two new shells out of her sequined bag.

Jessie fired on her with the rifle, but the shot went high, and it didn't even stop her forward progress.

A hail of bullets splintered the fence around them and sent the horses inside the corral into a white-eyed panic as they dashed around the pen. It was only the horses that saved them, the men shooting carefully so as to not hit any of the animals.

Jessie, still holding the repeater, ducked beneath the fence slats and ran for the animals. Cawdor was right behind her. A moment later, she had one by the halter and was running alongside it, her feet barely touching the ground as the panicked animal increased its speed. Cawdor was right behind her, grasping for another horse.

The shots halted for a moment, then Jessie heard Truesday yelling. "Kill them, you bastards! Damn the horses!"

Jessie's foot found the stirrup of the running horse and she pulled herself up. An instant later, she heard the shotgun's blast, then more shots. Spurring the horse on, she headed for the far side of the fence, hoping the horse could jump. Then she was sailing through the lead-filled air to make her escape.

As soon as she landed, she ventured a look behind. Cawdor was coming over the fence, but he'd been hit. A large red blossom of blood spread down from his left shoulder. He nearly fell as he landed, his chest falling to the mare's black mane. Then he uneasily recovered and they were galloping across the pasture, a dozen men in pursuit.

★

Chapter 11

"We should have stopped," Cawdor said. "We should have gotten Gathers."

"What we should have done is what we did—saved ourselves," Jessie said. "Gathers was dead before the second shot."

They were stopped at a small stand of trees, resting the horses. No doubt a posse was following them, but they'd have a small start. And Jessie wanted to look at Cawdor's shoulder. She didn't want him bleeding to death in the saddle.

"This isn't going to be good for us, is it?" Cawdor asked.

"Take off that shirt. We can talk about the rest later," Jessie instructed.

Cawdor obeyed, but he couldn't quite manage to work his fingers well enough to unbutton the shirt. Jessie helped with the buttons, then pulled down the badly bloodied garment gently.

The wound was bad, but Jessie had seen worse.

The bullet had sliced a neat groove into the flesh, high on Cawdor's arm.

Using water from the canteen, she washed the blood away and then ripped up his shirt to fashion a bandage from it. When she tied the length of torn shirt to his shoulder, she pulled it tight to stop the bleeding. If it kept bleeding right on through the material, she'd have to put a fire to it. And that was something she didn't care for, not at all.

They still had a long ride ahead of them and it wasn't going to be a pleasant one for Cawdor. "How's that feel?" Jessie asked, bringing her hands away and studying her handiwork with a critical eye.

"Fine, I guess," the young man said. Then, trying to move his shoulder about, he winced with pain.

"Try not moving it," Jessie suggested. "I can tie the whole arm down, but it wouldn't do much good in the saddle."

"I'll make it back to Delgado's, anyway," he said, then rose to climb back on his horse. Jessie had to help him with this, too.

Jessie had just put Cawdor in the saddle and was moving around to her own horse when she heard the sound. It could have been nothing, maybe a rabbit, but she froze in her tracks. A second later she heard the sound of a pistol cocking.

"Don't move, none of you both," the voice said.

Cawdor went for his gun and a shot kicked up a piece of dirt behind his horse, sending it into a panic that nearly threw him from the saddle.

"Don't move no more," the voice ordered.

Jessie brought her hands up and Cawdor followed suit, bringing one hand up.

"That's better," the voice announced.

Jessie turned and saw the young man come up from behind a dying bush not fifty yards away. "Who are you?" she asked. "What do you want?"

"Need to talk to you," the young man said.

"This your land?" Cawdor tried. "We're just passing through, if that's okay by you."

"Passing through," the young man snorted. "You're passing through, hell."

"We're strangers around here," Jessie said. "Trying to get downriver."

"Strangers, hell," the man said. "You're Cawdor Birnam and that Miss Starbuck."

"You don't have to take us back, you know," Jessie tried.

"I can make it worth your time to let us be on our way," Cawdor finished.

"Take you back, hell," came the answer. "I was gonna ask you to take me with you."

Jessie turned in the saddle to study the man. He was no more than a boy, really, but he was tall and thin, with a lean face that bespoke hard work and pale blue eyes that seemed incredibly young. He was nervous as a bird. Every movement he made seemed to be comprised of a series of twitches all strung together, as if he were a puppet with an amateur working the strings. And from the looks of him, he was the most scared of the three of them. "You're not part of Glamis's posse, are you?" she asked, looking him in the eye.

"I was part of it," he said, "but I ran away. After seeing what they did to that fella, that Ranger, you

113

can have my share of that kind of trouble."

Now it was Cawdor's turn to swivel in the saddle. "You don't work at the ranch," he said through a twinge of pain.

"Started day before yesterday," the young man answered. "Now I'm gonna put this gun away and I don't want you trying to kill me. That a bargain?"

Jessie nodded her agreement. When the young man turned to Cawdor, he nodded too.

"There ain't none of the old hands left—or nearly none," the young man answered, holstering the gun. "Glamis and his wife fired most of them. I was in town, broke as a three-wheeled wagon, and they signed me on. But I didn't sign on for killing no Ranger. Nobody told me that was in the bargain. Now you gonna take me with you?"

"Where's your horse?" Jessie asked.

"Broke her leg two miles back. Stepped in a hole," came the answer. "Had to shoot her. But I was running before that. Where you folks going, anyway? Hell, it don't matter, long as it's away from that ranch. Can't stand that kind of business, shooting folks, lawmen. That's bad business, any way you slice it. Where'd you say you were going? You didn't, did you? But that's fine, 'cause I'm not heading any place in particular anyways."

"Delgado's ranch, a day and a half ride," Cawdor said.

"This Delgado, they need a hand?" the young man answered.

"What's your name? Let's just start with your name, if that's fine by you?" Jessie asked.

"Kramer, Brit Kramer, ma'am," the young man answered. "Folks, they just call me Brit. They seem

114

to like it, 'cause on account of it being short and all. But it ain't short for nothing, understand, just Brit. That's what my ma and pa named me. Just like that, Brit."

"You figure you can walk and talk at the same time, Brit Kramer?" Cawdor asked.

"Figure I can, for awhile anyways," the young man replied.

"Then you turn over that gun and we'll start," Cawdor said, reaching out his good hand for the gun.

The young man pulled the pistol from the holster and handed it over without a trace of reluctance. "Let's start walking. Sooner we get there, the sooner I may have a job."

They started off slow, with the young man walking between the two horses. But they didn't go a dozen paces before Cawdor started asking questions.

"What's going on back there?" Cawdor asked.

Kramer, looking up, said, "I can't say what you'd call it, 'cause I never seen nothing like it. All the old hands, the ones that worked there before, Mr. Glamis fired 'em all, almost. The others he got out in line shacks and mending fence."

"Who were those others, the ones loafing when we got there?" Jessie asked.

"Hardcases from town and about," Kramer said. "Word went out that he was looking for men. Well, I didn't know what kind of men he was looking for when I signed up, but I reckon I found out fast enough. Too damned fast, if you ask me. I ain't no hardcase, understand, but I don't mind no hard work. Anyways, Mr. Glamis, he's paying them two dollars a day, plus room and board, to stand around and shoot what and who he tells them."

"Where'd they come from?" Cawdor asked. "I didn't see any faces I knew."

"Just started showing up," Kramer shrugged. "Showing up in ones and twos. I'll tell you for a fact, that work suits them. They'll shoot a man for two dollars a day, room and board. Do it quick, too. But that ain't the worst."

"What's the worst?" Jessie asked.

"Worst is that Truesday—Mrs. Glamis," the lad said, warming to the telling. "When she ain't bathing, she's yelling. They got one man, only job they gave him is heating water for her bathing. I swear, that lady takes eight, nine baths a day. Pours on this French perfume. Bought every damn bottle of it in town. Says she's washing the stink of cow off her. Ordered more from back east. Bathing and pouring on perfume, like she was getting paid good damned money for doing it, too. Rest of the time, she's going on about moving back north."

"She's leaving?" Cawdor asked. "Leaving Frank there by himself?"

"They're both of them leaving," Kramer said. "Selling the place off. Gonna sell it and move to Philadelphia. That's what they say. I believe 'em, too."

"Why's that?" Jessie asked.

" 'Cause they got ten men bringing the herd together," Kramer said. "That's what I signed on for. I was on my way out, horse and gear ready, when they called up the posse. I'll tell you, I just kept riding."

"They're looking to sell the land?" Cawdor asked.

"They're looking to sell everything," Kramer

116

answered. "Every piece of livestock down to the chickens, every inch of land, every saddle, every stick of furniture out of the house. Mrs. Glamis, she's saying she plans to leave Texas with nothing but money in her pocket. She says that she got the whole deal figured out, on paper, written down like. She's saying that the place is worth more sold off in bitty pieces than it is all put together like. That don't sound right to me, but she's got it all written down."

Jessie thought on it and knew that although it defied logic, it was probably true. It was like saying you could make more selling a watch off piece by piece than by selling the whole watch. But she'd seen ranches and land sold off in pieces and knew that Truesday Glamis was right.

"That ain't the strangest thing she got planned," Kramer said. "That ain't the strangest. Not by a long way. Know what the strangest thing is?"

"What's that?" Cawdor asked, the anger in him growing. He could picture Glamis selling off the ranch for pennies on the dollar. Every stockman for a hundred miles would ride in and buy a piece of it.

"She's talking about going to Paris in France," Kramer added, his voice more than a little shocked. "Now, why'd anyone want to do something like that? That just ain't a sane person talking."

Jessie had been to France and Paris, at that. Aside from the food, the people, the cities, and the weather, she didn't mind it all that much.

By late afternoon, Cawdor let Kramer ride for awhile. They would have to go easy on the horses, but the young man had offered information so freely that Cawdor figured that he deserved to ride at least part of the way. Maybe, Cawdor figured, that riding would quiet him down a bit. Probably the young hand deserved a job as well. He'd talk to Miranda about taking him on.

They made camp that night by the river. Luckily, Kramer had brought some food along, packed for his work and escape. It wasn't much, a few biscuits and some smoked beef, but it was better than nothing. Briefly, Jessie thought of trying to shoot a rabbit, but then thought better of it. A fire might attract the attention of the posse, if they were still tracking them.

"I'll tell you," Kramer said, biting into a biscuit. "Those cattle, what I saw, they're fine looking animals. Going be worth some money, altogether."

"Where they putting them?" Jessie asked, chewing on a slice of beef.

"Bringing them all into the near pasture," Kramer answered. "Not much to graze, for what, three hundred head?"

"Three twenty-five," Cawdor mumbled.

Kramer nodded, then said, "But they're putting out all the winter hay. Should have them all together in another few days. They sent a man into town to put out posters, send telegraphs and such. Probably by next week there won't be a head left on the property."

Jessie saw a flash of disgust and anger cross Cawdor's face. He was letting his temper get the best of him again. Jessie knew that if they were to do anything about the situation, she'd have to keep him from doing something stupid. Most particularly, she'd have to keep him from doing something that would get him killed. That alone would be a full-time, sunup to sundown job.

"Know what I should do?" Cawdor asked.

"What's that?" Kramer answered. "I know what I would do, damn straight. But I ain't good at guessing other people. Never have been, suspect I can't hope to be, ever. So, tell me, what's that you should do?"

"Should ride back there and just put a bullet in Glamis," Cawdor said. "Shoot that bastard like the mad dog he is. Shoot him deader than hell."

"Can't argue with that," Kramer said. "That man's head don't work right."

"You'd be dead before you got within a mile of the place," Jessie reasoned. "He let that Ranger get close enough and got his brain nearly bashed in. You think he's gonna let you walk into his parlor and shoot him?"

"My parlor, damn it!" Cawdor corrected heatedly.

"That's right, your parlor," Jessie answered. "But right now he's standing in it and you won't get within a mile of it if you try riding back there."

"Can't argue with that," Kramer said. "She's making a lot of sense, if you ask me. What with you being shot up and all, they'd pick you off like a varmint."

"Now, what you need is a plan," Jessie said soothingly. "And a good one."

Cawdor chewed a piece of beef angrily. He chewed it like he was chewing on Glamis's heart. "You wouldn't happen to have one of those handy, would you now?"

"That's right," Kramer put in. "A plan sounds like a damn fine idea."

"Let's just get back to Delgado. Maybe he can help us out on that count," Jessie said. "And if you don't mind now, Mr. Kramer, we're just going to tie you up for the night."

"Why's that?"

"Well, just supposing you aren't who you say you are and aren't what you say you are, then maybe it'll keep you from slitting our throats when we sleep."

Kramer thought on this for a full minute, then put his hands out in front of him. "That might be a good idea," he said at last.

They set out early in the morning after untying Kramer. With any luck, they'd reach Delgado's before noon. It felt strange to be traveling back again. Strange and unproductive was how Jessie saw it. Yet it was necessary. To try facing down the hired guns who protected Glamis would be like putting a gun to their heads. And the sheriff, well, he was more than likely bought and paid for. Jessie briefly thought of trying another rancher, but then they couldn't be trusted either, at least not now. Not with the sell-off coming soon. Every rancher within fifty miles was probably looking to buy at least some of the cheap cattle. And those who had land near the Birnam property were probably looking to divide up the land. The only people they could trust were at Delgado's now.

"Well, you got that plan yet?" Cawdor asked at midmorning.

"I'm thinking on it," Jessie replied. "Best thing we can do now is talk to Miranda and Ki. See what they think."

"It's easy for you to preach patience when it's not

your land Glamis stole," Cawdor complained.

Jessie was about to answer something mean and low, but thought better of it. "Cawdor, don't worry," she said finally. "I won't let anything happen to your land or the cattle, for that matter."

He smiled a grim little smile and said, "This whole deal, it just isn't right."

"I know, but we're going to put it right," Jessie said with a note of reassurance in her voice.

"Know what I'd like to see?" Kramer asked. He was sitting up behind Cawdor and had been since they started out. Him walking would slow down the whole deal.

Neither Jessie nor Cawdor answered the young man. More than likely, he'd like to see some whiskey and women. Maybe he just wanted to see another job.

"Know what I would surely like to see?" Kramer asked again, his voice pleading for a response.

"What's that?" Jessie answered at last, mainly just to keep him from asking again. Kramer had fallen asleep the night before, exhausted but still talking. That morning, he'd gotten up early, rising from a dead sleep, talking, and he hadn't quit since.

"I would purely like to see all of them three hundred head—" he started.

"Three twenty-five," Cawdor corrected.

"—All of them three hundred and twenty-five head running hell-bent stampeding over every one of those mean sons of bitches on the property. Now that would purely be something to see, wouldn't it?"

121

"That would be something," Cawdor answered, dispirited.

"Wouldn't it?" Kramer repeated, awaiting an answer from Jessie.

"It would," she said, but without enthusiasm.

★

Chapter 12

They reached the Delgado ranch late in the afternoon. Kramer had slowed them down some, but not much. Mostly, he had just talked their ears off with foolishness. Sometime just before they crossed the property line, Cawdor had threatened to shoot the young man. "Nobody that ever met you would say I was wrong," Cawdor cautioned. The threat silenced the lad for less than three minutes. He was just one of those people who needed to talk. He needed it like other people needed to breathe and eat.

No hidden gunmen greeted Jessie and Cawdor as they approached the ranch. Coming in over the fertile pasture, the place seemed oddly dead. Even the cattle, grazing peacefully, appeared subdued.

As they came closer, Jessie saw that even the balcony, where the old man kept his careful eye on the place, was empty.

"You get the feeling something's wrong?" Jessie asked.

"Damn quiet place, ain't it?" Kramer said.

"Too damn quiet," Cawdor answered as they approached the barn.

"Let's just see to the horses, then find out what's going on," Jessie said.

"That one of your plans?" Cawdor sneered as he started for the barn.

Jessie ignored him and stepped down off the horse. Kramer followed and then helped Cawdor down. She was glad to reach the ranch, just to have a doctor look at Cawdor's shoulder. The shoulder needed looking after, but the young man needed something that nobody could pack into a poultice.

The three of them led the horses into the barn, stepping into the darkness silently. It wasn't until they'd just passed completely into the building that Jessie heard the rustle.

"Just hold it right there," a voice commanded.

The three of them froze.

A moment later, seven men with guns stepped out of the stalls, stood up behind hay bales, and appeared in the loft. All of the men wore the same icy expression, as if shooting them meant as little as killing a fly.

Jessie's hand instinctively went for her gun. Then a voice behind her said, "Don't try it, lady; Texas Rangers."

Jessie's hand froze, halfway to the gun, and as her eyes grew accustomed to the light, she saw that indeed, all the men were wearing Texas Ranger badges.

"Now, if this don't just beat all," Kramer said. "You boys are just the fellas we want to see."

"I wouldn't be so sure of that," the Ranger behind them said as he stepped up and removed Jessie's gun from her holster. "Jessica Starbuck and Cawdor Birnam, you're under arrest for the murder of Ranger Gathers."

The next part, well, that was just like a nightmare. The Rangers formed a loose circle around Jessie, Cawdor, and Kramer and marched them back into the house.

"You know about that job I was talking about, maybe I should just be on my way," Kramer said.

"Shut it up, son," one of the Rangers commanded and nudged the youth along with a shotgun. "You just keep talking and you're going to force me to do something neither of us wants me to do."

The walk back to the house seemed to take forever, but it was the longest she'd ever heard Kramer silent. In the parlor were Miranda, Ki, and the old man. Apparently he'd gotten his rope contraption on the stairs working.

All the Rangers but one positioned themselves at the doors. The remaining lawman, whom Jessie took to be the leader, sat in one of the large chairs in the living room to hear their version of the story, a confession, or whatever else they chose to say. Jessie could tell, just by looking at the trail-weary Ranger, that he was hoping for a confession, but not counting on it terribly hard. He had that look of a man trying to fill an inside straight, but not looking to bet on it.

"It wouldn't put any of you out too much to tell me what exactly is going on here, would it?" Jessie asked.

The Rangers looked at each other as if she'd just asked if it were night or day. "It's like this," the tallest of the Texas lawmen said. "We got word that

125

a Ranger was killed down at the Glamis ranch."

"It's not the Glamis ranch yet!" Cawdor spat. "It's not his yet. It won't ever be his."

The lawman ignored the outburst. "Well, we knew he was riding down this way, to check out something on the ranch, so we just figured we'd stop down here, seeing as this is where you folks seemed to be holed up."

"And just who sent you this word?" Jessie asked. "It wouldn't have been Glamis, would it?"

"Sent us word and the body," the Ranger offered with a slow nod. "Both came straight from the Glamis spread."

"And you believed that lying bastard?" Cawdor snorted.

The Ranger cocked his head to one side. "That ain't exactly a hard question, son," he said. "You're asking if I believe a ranch owner's word over that of a man wanted for the murder of his own pa and for rustling."

"I didn't kill my pa!"

"I didn't say you did, just that you're wanted for it," the Ranger countered. "But I got a pretty good feeling you and this lady broke out of the lockup. Now, that rustling charge, that just seems a might small, in light of all the others."

Jessie, seeing that someone had to take charge, asked, "What exactly did Glamis say? What's his side to what went on back there?"

"Told me that you and this fella here rode into the ranch with guns blazing," the Ranger answered. "He was out back talking to Gathers, and you folks just gunned him down like a dog. Had a signed and sworn statement from a

126

half-dozen men saying that's exactly the way it happened."

"That ain't the way it happened at all!" Kramer broke in. "I seen the whole thing. Seen it all!"

"Now, who would you be?" the Ranger asked.

"Name's Kramer," the boy answered. "Up to a couple days ago I worked on the Glamis ranch. And I seen the whole thing. Seen it from start to end. And that ain't the way it happened, the way you said."

"I told them that you left with Gathers," Miranda said suddenly. "They didn't believe me."

"Even if I did believe you, that don't mean I believe them," the Ranger offered. "Now son, why don't you just tell me your side of it."

Kramer inhaled deeply, fueling himself for the story. "I signed on as a hand, see?" he began. "Well, I'm there just a day or two, and they send me out to check the stock in the summer pasture, see. Normally I don't favor that kind of work. Don't like lonely work. Not at all. Nobody to talk to, see. I'm a social type. Riding the fence don't bother me, that ain't lonely. But checking stock, well, that's lonely work. Don't favor it, not at all. But a job's a job—"

"What did you see?" the Ranger asked, annoyed. "Just tell us what you saw."

"Now I'm in the barn, getting my bag and such ready, and I hear kind of a commotion. So I sneak up to the door. I figure it's some of the boys, having it out over something. But it ain't no such thing. What it is, is that Ranger, Gathers, beating the holy hell out of Mr. Glamis."

"Gathers was beating on Mr. Glamis?" the Ranger asked warily.

"Yes sir," Kramer said. "Beating on him something awful. Then Mrs. Glamis, she let into him with a shotgun, both barrels. Nearly cut him clean in half. I'll tell you, I don't ever hope to see nothing like that ever again."

"Mrs. Glamis shot Gathers?" the lawman asked.

Looking around the room, Jessie could see nothing but disbelief on everyone's face. She wondered what her own face showed. She wouldn't have believed the story either, not unless she'd seen it herself.

"Yes sir, both barrels," Kramer answered quickly. "Didn't even think about it. Well, sir, I seen that and I knew I didn't want any truck with those folks."

"And that's when you met up with these folks?" the lawman asked.

"Yes sir, but I didn't know anything about that one there murdering his pa," Kramer added quickly in his defense. "There a reward or anything posted for them?"

"Why you ask?" the Ranger said.

"Just 'cause, you know, officially speaking, maybe, I was the one that brought them back," Kramer answered.

The last bit was too much for Cawdor; in a flash he was out of the chair, his hands around Kramer's throat. Calmly, one of the Rangers stepped forward and knocked Cawdor cold with the butt of his shotgun.

It was a couple of hours before Cawdor began to stir. Jessie figured that with all the blood that leaked out of him and the few sleepless nights he'd spent, the Ranger's tap with the scattergun provided some needed sleep. In any event, the sleep allowed

128

Jessie to dress his wounds and to have a couple of the lawmen carry him up the stairs to a bedroom without a fight.

"What happened, exactly?" he asked, even before opening his eyes.

"Got knocked out by a Texas Ranger," Jessie said, sitting on the edge of the bed, letting her fingers lightly stroke his brow.

"Oh lordy, did I kill that little turd, Kramer?"

A small smile spread across Jessie's face. "Not even close," she answered.

Cawdor's face changed to a pained look. "I am just not having a good day," he groaned and shut his eyes again.

"Truthfully, I could probably say I've had better days, too," she answered. Jessie could have told him that Kramer eventually talked himself out and that all his talk eventually wore down the Rangers. Whether they could pick the truth out of the story he told was another matter, but Jessie felt it was likely that they had seen at least a portion of truth in it. After all, a man couldn't talk that much without touching on the truth at least once or twice.

Then, bending down just a little, she kissed Cawdor lightly on the lips.

She'd expected him to drift back off into sleep, but instead, he brought his arms up, encircling her waist and back and drawing her closer to him as their lips pressed closer together in a passionate kiss.

Jessie eased herself up into the bed and he drew her closer. As their lips reluctantly parted, he brought a hand down to the front and began unbuttoning her shirt.

"Are you sure this is a good idea?" she whispered

in his ear. "There's a Ranger guarding the door."

"Probably the best idea I've had all day," he whispered back as he slid his hand inside her shirt to gently massage her breast.

Well, she couldn't argue with him on that count. Lately, it seemed that neither of them had come up with any good ideas. Yes, that, and the fact that his thumb, slowing teasing her nipple to pert hardness, just felt so damn good.

Shrugging, Jessie let the shirt fall from her soft shoulders, revealing both of her wonderfully firm breasts. Cawdor eased himself up and took the closest tender globe to his face, feeling its solid warmth against his skin. His three-day beard tickled her harshly. Then, turning his head, the young man opened his mouth and let the already hardened nipple slide smoothly between his full lips.

Jessie shook her head, her hair falling back over her shoulders, as she abandoned her lovely breasts to Cawdor's tender ministrations. His smooth, hot tongue circled the hard little nipple again and again, sending quivering warmth shooting through her.

When Cawdor judged himself finished with one nipple, he abandoned it to the cool air and set his tongue's ardent affections on the other.

Jessie leaned back, resting her head on the thick pillow, as Cawdor lifted the mound of soft flesh to his mouth.

Reaching out, she let her fingers trail over the thick mat of hair on his chest, feeling the muscles tighten, then relax under her slow-handed touch. Then, very slowly, she allowed her fingers to play down his body, exploring it blindly and thrilling to each new surface.

Finally, her hand reached his hard, washboard stomach. Resting her hand lightly on his stomach, she inched her way forward, teasing herself as much as him, until she felt the thick, dark hair that encompassed her lustful destination.

Cawdor brought a short breath in and continued to tease her nipple as she let her fingertips trail around the dark man-hair surrounding his member.

The young man released Jessie's breast from his mouth, sending it tingling and puckering in the cool air, and wiggled his good arm downward, until it was resting on her upper thigh. Jessie squeezed it tightly between her strong legs and allowed her fingers to explore lower, between his legs, brushing his most sensitive and forbidden places as lightly as a feather.

Soon, she could stand his gentle teasing no longer. Coming upright, she had her boots and pants off in a flash, then resumed her position. Now, she could feel the heat of his body against her long legs under the covers. Bringing her hand back to his shaft, she grasped it firmly at the base, while her fingers played a gentle tattoo up and down its underside.

Moving slowly downward, she positioned herself so that she was kneeling between her legs. Holding his shaft in two hands, she glanced upward to look at him. He was as fine-looking a man as she had ever had, and as strong, too. Yet, something about his bandaged shoulder gave him a helpless look, arousing sympathy as well as lust in her.

Bowing her head, she took the entire length of his shaft slowly into her mouth, letting it slide smoothly in, in one sensuous downward stroke. She held it there for a long time, feeling its warmth and hardness filling her. Then, slowly, slowly, she lifted her head, allowing the shaft to slip gleaming from between her full, pouting lips.

When the shaft was nearly entirely out of her mouth, she held just the very top of it solidly between her lips and let her tongue run a smooth circle around and around. Then, nodding her head forward more, she released the shaft from its warm, wet refuge and brought her tongue out to lick the entire underside.

Cawdor let out a long moan of pleasure, his good hand reaching down to toy gently with Jessie's breasts. He took the still-hardened nipple between thumb and forefinger and gently rolled it this way and that, like winding a clock with unimaginable delicacy.

With each touch of his hand on her breast, Jessie felt a new wave of pleasure flow through her body. Lifting her head, she once again engulfed the entire length of the shaft, letting it sink slowly into her mouth as her tongue teased every inch of it.

Edging up in bed, Cawdor brought his hand drifting downward, his fingers grazing along her smooth, pale legs. Then he was touching her silken thatch, his fingers teasing the hair, combing it ever so lightly, then pulling. Jessie spread her legs wider, inviting the teasing fingers inside. And when they would not enter, she crouched lower.

When she could stand his teasing no longer, she released his shaft from her mouth and positioned herself over it. Cawdor studied her with a sly smile and half-closed eyes as she grabbed his shaft again and guided it into her.

Jessie began raising and lowering herself

immediately, the slick shaft sliding smoothly and delightfully in and out. With each stroke, she moved faster, until she had to make herself slow the pace for fear of hurting Cawdor's injured arm.

Resting her hands on his strong thighs, she moved up and down, grinding the long member into her, feeling her breasts bouncing delightfully in time to her motions, until, finally, she felt herself reaching her moment. She could control herself no longer. Coming up and down faster and faster, they raced together toward release as Cawdor let out a low moan of pleasure and pain.

Again, they reached their moment together as long, shuddering waves of pleasure shot through them and they sent the iron springs supporting the bed singing.

When they finished, Jessie collapsed forward, his shaft still inside her. Turning his face toward her, he kissed her long and hard, as his muscular chest crushed her breasts. They were both breathing hard, their hearts beating so fast, she feared they might explode from the joy of it.

Later, they were both sitting up in bed, watching the last of the sunlight come slanting in through the curtained window. Jessie turned to Cawdor and said, "This is just one helluva mess."

"I suppose it is," he answered lazily. "But somehow I don't feel that bad about it."

"Now why would that be?" she asked squirming away slightly and coming up on one elbow to study his face. Oddly, he was smiling, just a little, but smiling. For the life of her, she could not figure why he would not be gun-to-the-head low feeling.

133

The last couple of days had been just that bad, at least from her way of thinking.

"Well, for one thing, I got a plan," he said lazily.

"It better be a good one," she replied.

"Well, it's not really a plan yet," he said. "It's like an idea for a plan."

Jessie felt herself tighten with fear. An "idea for a plan" was often worse than no plan at all. "You want to tell me about it?" she asked warily.

"It's like this," he said and turned so that he was facing her. "We escape, go back to the property, and run that bastard and his men off."

"And?"

"Well, I haven't worked out all the particulars yet," Cawdor answered.

"Have you worked out any of the particulars?"

"Well, no, not exactly," the young man admitted. "But it's a start."

"It may be a bad one," Jessie said.

"What could be worse than where we are now? We're out of any kind of options at all."

"Being dead is worse," Jessie said. "Being dead kind of narrows your options."

★

Chapter 13

Jessie opened the door a crack and saw the Ranger guarding the way. She didn't have to look far; he was sitting next to the door, the chair blocking most of the doorway and his legs extending out across the path.

It was late and he was sleeping, but even then, escape seemed impossible. Edging back into the room, she walked across toward the window where Cawdor was standing. Two more Rangers walked guard duty in the courtyard.

"Not through the door, not out through the window," Jessie said.

"No, not at all," Cawdor answered, letting the drapery fall back into place. "Good night for it though, moon's clouded over. Can't see but a few stars."

Jessie stretched out on the bed. She would be content to await word from the governor's office. But by then it could well be too late to save the Birnam ranch. "Let's just wait them out," Jessie suggested hopelessly.

135

"Jessie, I'm shocked and surprised," Cawdor said. "A woman of action like you, wanting to wait the bastards out."

There was something in Cawdor's voice that worried her. He somehow didn't seem worried. Maybe it was the wound—all the blood he'd lost— or the sex, but he appeared almost as giddy as a schoolgirl. He couldn't have worried her more if he'd returned to his murderous vengeance mood. After all, he wasn't talking about busting out of some breadbox jail. He was planning to escape a half dozen Rangers armed with repeaters and shotguns.

"See, I do believe I have a plan," he said at last.

Jessie sat up on the bed. "It better be a good one," she answered. "These Rangers aren't playing, not even a little bit."

"Oh, it's good," Cawdor said. "Damn good."

Against her will, Jessie felt herself becoming infected with his enthusiasm for escape. A small smile parted her lips and she cocked an eyebrow to ask about the plan.

"Can't go out through the door, right?"

She nodded.

"Can't go out through that window, right?"

Again she nodded.

"Only thing left is straight up," Cawdor said, and let his gaze wander up to the ceiling.

Jessie followed his gaze. The timbers must have been an inch thick beneath the clay tile shingles outside. Delgado built the house to last. He'd built it for his grandchildren to raise their children in. "I don't know," Jessie said, but she kept studying the ceiling.

"We pry them off," Cawdor answered. "Two lengths

136

and we can slip out, run across the roof, and drop down by the stables."

Jessie kept staring, unconvinced.

"Only thing is, we'd need tools," Cawdor said.

"An ax wouldn't hurt," she said. "I can just wake up that Ranger out there and ask for one."

Cawdor made a sour face. "Why don't you just help me pile this furniture up," he scolded. "Chair on the dresser should do it. And turn down that light."

Jessie turned down the light, as the young man placed the heavy mission chair on the dresser's wide top. Then she watched Cawdor, his arm hurting, climb up on the chair. He reached the ceiling easily. Cawdor pushed hard with his good hand. Nothing moved.

"Damn, but old Delgado built this place well," he swore.

"He wasn't that old when he built it," Jessie answered as she stood with her arms across her chest.

Cawdor stood there temporarily stymied as he studied the entire expanse of the ceiling. "Maybe not that well," he said at last, a small trace of hope creeping into his voice.

Jessie followed his gaze to a small water stain near the door. It might have been just a minute leak or it could have been rotting planks, long neglected.

Coming awkwardly down from his perch, Cawdor positioned himself behind the dresser. "Help me move this big bastard," he said, straining his good arm.

They moved the dresser with some difficulty, the legs screeching on the floor. If the guard could hear at all, he would hear that. Jessie was about to say

137

something about the noise, but Cawdor was already scampering up on the chair.

"Hold the damned table," he ordered as he stood to his full height on the chair.

Jessie was halfway around the table when the door burst open.

Cawdor panicked, lost his footing, and began to fall the moment the guard looked in. The Ranger began to say something that began, "What the hell—" when Cawdor, all two hundred and some odd pounds, fell full on him just as he brought the repeater up.

The sudden blow knocked the wind out of the Ranger and Jessie pulled the rifle from his grasp as Cawdor lay moaning alongside. "I never hoped to hit a Ranger, and I'm real sorry for this time," Jessie said as she closed the door. She smashed the rifle down alongside the man's head, knocking him cold.

"Was that part of your plan, too?" Jessie asked, helping Cawdor up.

"Can't say it was, but it worked just fine, too," Cawdor answered as he came to his feet. He was still in considerable pain from his shoulder. Jessie could see he was trying to talk around it.

"We got one chance," Jessie said. "You change clothes with this old boy, right now!"

Cawdor did as he was told, then tied the Ranger up with bed sheets.

When he was done, Cawdor pulled the Ranger's hat down over his eyes and stepped slowly into the hall. Two more Rangers sat in chairs below, near the entranceway, sleeping. He walked slowly down the hall to Ki's room where a Ranger slept in a chair outside the door.

"Rise and shine," Cawdor whispered, as he stuck the Colt under the man's chin.

For the briefest moment, the guard began to cry out, then thought better of it. A moment later, they had passed soundlessly into Ki's room.

Ki, already fully dressed, as if waiting, said, "Ah."

It took less than five minutes to tie the guard to the bed with a gag planted firmly over his mouth.

"We must find Rosalie," Ki said. "And Miranda."

Moving soundlessly, Ki and Cawdor crept back along the hallway to where Jessie was waiting.

"They must be on the other side," she said. "No way to reach them."

"I have an idea," Ki said.

Ten minutes later, Jessie opened the door to the old man's room. Apparently the Rangers thought a man was not necessary to guard a cripple.

Creeping into the dark room, she heard his labored breathing. With any luck at all, she would not awaken him. Moving out to the balcony, she checked the length of rope she'd cut from the old man's wheelchair lift, and watched as the two guards moved into the shadows, talking in low voices.

She climbed carefully up on the balcony's railing, then, reaching up, grabbed the edge of the roof. Pulling as hard as she could, she brought her feet up off the railing and swung hard, so that her boot caught the edge. Hesitating a moment, fearing the guards, she pulled again, rolling up onto the roof. A minute later, she was running along the tiles toward the chimney. The chimney was a low, squat thing made of adobe. If it didn't hold her weight and more, they'd all be dead.

Making two half-hitches around the chimney, she played out the rope and waited, crouching on the roof in the darkness, her breathing coming fast. The minutes ticked by slowly. Then, after what seemed hours, she heard the first shots. The bullets, culled from one of the Rangers' repeaters, sounded distant and hollow as they exploded in the fireplace, but they still sounded like shots.

Guns leveled, the two guards ran from the shadows into the house. The instant they vanished, Jessie moved to the edge of the roof, brought the rope from around her neck, and tossed it over the side. Then, lowering herself down, she paused near the window and swung out, kicking it in with a boot heel.

Miranda and Rosalie appeared in the broken window immediately, their faces painted with panic and questions.

"Come on, now!" Jessie ordered.

Neither woman had to be told twice. Rosalie crawled through the window, grabbed the twisting rope in both hands just beneath Jessie, and slid to the ground. A second later, Miranda began to follow.

"Not you," Jessie said. Jessie released one hand from the rope, reached out, and punched Miranda hard, sending her falling back into the darkened room. By morning she'd have a nice bruise along her cheek, which should convince the Rangers that she'd been overpowered.

Jessie half slid and half fell to earth seconds after Rosalie. She'd done her part; now, if only Cawdor and Ki had made good their escape. Racing across the courtyard, she received her answer. There, beyond the portico, sitting on two fresh horses and holding another two by the reins, were Ki and Cawdor.

Jessie and Rosalie ran for the mounts. They fairly leapt into saddles as they grabbed the reins and galloped off. By the time they reached the fence, they heard the first shots from the Rangers' repeaters. Jessie felt one of the bullets streak hotly past her cheek, but she kept going.

"They'll be after us, any second," Jessie yelled ahead to Cawdor.

"I cut their saddle cinches," he called back. "It'll take awhile for them to notice," he answered back, his words whipping past Jessie's ears in the wind.

They rode for what seemed like hours at a full gallop. It was, Jessie surmised, a miracle that none of them had been killed or run the horses to death. But by the time they slowed, they were well away from the ranch. No doubt the Rangers were on their trail, but they would need at least a little daylight to track them properly. And for three more hours at least, they owned the night.

"Where we head now, Mexico?" Rosalie asked.

Jessie turned to her, noticing for the first time that she was wearing a nightgown.

"Back to the Birnam ranch," Jessie said.

"Oh, no," Rosalie answered. "I ain't going back there; them people are crazier than you folks."

"You can head on back to the Rangers then," Cawdor suggested.

"Not me, they want to kill me," she answered. "I told them what went on and they didn't believe me. Didn't believe me any more than they believed that boy, Kramer."

"I just don't see where you have a whole bunch of choices to make," Cawdor said. "You just escaped from the Texas Rangers. Those boys don't take kindly to that particular sort of activity—makes 'em look bad. And Texas Rangers, they just hate like hell to look bad."

"Well, I hate like hell to be dead," she snapped back. "You hear what I'm telling you, Mr. Birnam."

"Come back with us, Rosalie," Ki said gently. "I will not let any harm come to you. It is your best choice."

"Ki, you're a fine fella," she said. "But really, are you in a position to be making promises like that and all?"

"Yes," Ki answered simply, then turned his attention to the trail ahead.

"Just hang it all," Rosalie said. "Teaches me for going against my better thinking. Young ladies shouldn't ever be sliding out of windows on ropes at unlawful hours in their nighties."

They all had to laugh at that, which was good, because they all knew that maybe it would be the last laugh they'd have for a long time to come.

★

Chapter 14

They came down off their horses behind a small hill and worked their way up to the crest on their bellies. As they reached the top, Jessie, Ki, Cawdor, and Rosalie saw for themselves that Kramer had not been lying. The pasture lay empty before them.

"Must be they plan on selling off the stock soon," Cawdor mused. "There isn't enough hay to last more than a couple days for three hundred head."

"Three hundred and twenty-five," Jessie corrected.

Cawdor gave her an annoyed look, then turned his attention back to the empty pasture.

"It never occurred to you to steal a gun or two, did it?" Rosalie asked. "I mean I could see where that would be a real advantage against twenty-five men with guns."

"No, I suppose in all the confusion and all, we just forgot," Cawdor said. "However, I do have a plan."

Jessie turned her head, ear against the ground, to study his face. "Hope it's a good one, Cawdor," she said.

"Don't go worrying about that," he replied. "We just got to get us a couple of weapons. Revolvers would be best."

"Myself, I'd like a Sharps buffalo gun. A big fifty," Rosalie put in. "That is, if you're taking orders for them now."

"Look," Ki said.

All of them turned their attentions back to the pasture. It took Jessie a long time, but finally she saw what Ki had seen. Far off, a speck moved in the sun-baked distance. Then the speck shifted slightly and became two specks.

"Riders, two of them," Cawdor announced.

"What are they doing? They couldn't have seen us," Rosalie whispered and brought her body closer to the ground.

"Gathering up the cow shit, maybe," Cawdor said. "If they plan on selling the breeding stock and all, that's the only thing left."

"Probably sent out after any strays," Jessie answered. "My guess is that Glamis doesn't want to leave a dime's worth of beef on the land."

The four of them watched as the men came closer, riding stirrup to stirrup at a lazy pace.

"Heading up to winter pasture," Cawdor said. "Searching out along the river."

"What do you think, Ki?" Jessie asked. "Can you get their guns and horses?"

"Perhaps," came the modest answer. "I can only say perhaps. I will need a weapon. I have but one *shuriken* left."

"Well, if we had weapons, then you wouldn't need one, would you?" Rosalie quipped.

But both Jessie and Cawdor knew what he meant.

It seemed sometimes to Jessie that almost anything could become a weapon in Ki's expert hands. "There's a patch of scrub oak back there," she said. "But you better hurry."

A moment later, Ki had eased himself back down the hill and was running easily for the trees while the other three continued to watch the approach of the two riders.

When the pair of riders were within half a mile, Ki came back up the hill, holding a long, stout branch broken off from a tree. It was nearly shoulder height and he held it like a staff as he walked briskly back up the hill.

"They're getting damn close," Rosalie said, backing up a little.

Ki approached them, crouching. Coming to the top of the hill, within sight of the riders, he began to dance, spinning slowly so that the staff was raised up slightly and his other hand was in the air. Jessie's practiced eye saw the glint of a throwing star in the free hand as Ki danced over the crest.

Rosalie stared wide-eyed, as if she knew for a fact that Ki was crazy as a pet coon. But when neither of her other two companions reacted, she held her tongue.

Ki danced crazily down the hill, remarkably keeping his balance as he swung the stick high over his head, then brought it around his waist.

The four of them watched as the two horsemen stopped. One removed a filthy, low-crowned white hat and scratched his head. Both kept their hands near their gunbelts. Jessie knew that had they encountered Ki simply walking along, they would have shot him on sight. But here, out in front of

145

them, was a tall Oriental with a big stick, dancing down a hill in the middle of the afternoon. Their curiosity had gotten the better of them, or simply, the task ahead was so boring that they longed for a diversion of any type—even a crazy man.

Ki let out a loud yell and continued dancing, moving straight for the two riders, the stick swinging wildly in the air.

"They're gonna shoot him," Rosalie gasped. "They're gonna shoot him quick."

"No, they won't," Jessie whispered back. "By the time they figure it out, it'll be too late."

Ki danced faster, now moving between the two horsemen as he danced and cavorted merrily.

One of the riders reined his horse out of the way, so as to give the crazy man more room. The other one said something, but the words were lost in the distance.

Suddenly, in a flash, Ki moved the stick back above his head, bringing the tip within an inch of first one horse's eye, then the other's. Both animals shied slightly, tossing their heads and prancing away. As the riders pulled up on the reins, Ki struck.

The stick came out fast, jabbing gracefully but forcefully into one rider's ribs and knocking him from the saddle. As the other rider went for his gun, Ki spun around and shot his arm out, throwing the star into the man's neck. A great gout of blood spouted from the severed artery, but Ki was already gone, moving around the front of the first man's horse, where the rider lay on the ground. In a flash, he had the reins and was dealing a death blow across the rider's skull as the downed horseman went for his pistol.

Jessie, Cawdor, and Rosalie were up and running wildly down the hill. The rider with the *shuriken* in his neck was slumped over the saddle, his fist locked around the horn in a death grip. The horse was wide-eyed and in a panic. The reins hung down loosely across its neck, and its mane was covered in quarts of thick, warm blood.

Jessie grabbed the reins of the dead man's horse and brought it under control as the rider fell heavily to the ground.

Cawdor caught the other horse with one hand along the bridle and began to soothe it. "What do you have there?" he called to Jessie. "I got myself a ten-gauge shotgun and two ivory-handled Smith & Wessons."

"Colt side arm and a new repeater in the boot," she called back.

Rosalie, unable to control herself, threw her arms around Ki and kissed him full on the lips. "That was wonderful," she shouted, bringing her face away. "Wonderful."

"If you think that was wonderful," Cawdor called to Rosalie, "wait till you hear my plan."

"I'd like to hear about this plan that you dreamed up, too," Jessie said. "And it better be good."

"Oh, it's good," Cawdor answered without a trace of modesty in his voice. "But let me say I'd like to share just a little of the credit with Kramer. He's the one who gave me the idea."

They rode to the ranch at dusk, doubling up the horses. When they were within a half mile of the ranch, Jessie and Ki stepped down and headed in opposite directions.

All of them moved quickly. Jessie knew that she and Ki would have to be in their places by the time the first shots were fired. With the heavy Colt strapped around her waist, she looked over and watched as Ki vanished at a trot over a hill. It was one of the few times she'd ever seen him wearing a gun. The heavy gunbelt looked strange around his slim waist.

After a few minutes of walking, the herd came into sight. It was in the pasture nearest the house. The cows were grouped in tightly and moving stiffly in the twilight. They bowed their heads, grazing, but already, even after no more than a couple of days, the grass was nearly grazed out. The herd was probably scheduled to be sold soon, perhaps even the next day.

Jessie spotted the first guards at the fence line. There were two of them, holding their repeaters casually and leaning against the fence, smoking. Jessie faded back, waiting for an opportunity.

Then, close by, she heard the first shots. A small movement ran through the herd, nothing to speak of, just a nervous shifting. Then more shots followed, and the cows surged forward.

The two men came off the fence and began to run for the house, rifles out in front. Jessie came up and yelled, "Hold it there!"

The pair spun, almost at the same time, bringing up their guns. Jessie fired twice, hitting both men in the chest and sending them spinning back toward the fence. Her shots turned the herd in on itself. Running forward, she grabbed up both their guns and began firing into the air as she ran alongside the wall of running cattle, turning strays back into the herd.

More shots were coming now from all around. It

was difficult to know who was shooting, but the herd was stampeding, running hell-bent for the house. The air was filled with dust, the noise deafening and the ground shaking beneath Jessie's boots.

Now she could distinctly hear shots coming from the front. Shotguns, pistols, and rifles were drowned out by the stampede. Again and again, Jessie found to her panic that she was nearly engulfed by the cattle and had to run a wide arc to keep clear of the herd.

Then, right in front of her, she saw another gunman. He was standing at the side, firing in the air, trying to turn the sea of cattle away. Spotting Jessie, he fired in her direction and missed. Running in fast, she dropped one repeater and fired the other from the hip. Through the dust, she saw the top of the gunman's head explode just beneath the hairline.

Ahead was the house, no more than a shadow looming up in front of the running cattle. Two more gunmen appeared. Jessie shot the first as he raised a pistol. The second panicked, ran into the herd, and was trampled, his screams muted in the thunder of the cattle.

For an instant, the stampede halted as the cattle came to the fences. Then more gunshots rang out from the rear and the herd moved ahead, crashing through the fences and on toward the house. Now, as she ran alongside, Jessie saw the bodies, hardly recognizable anymore, of those who had tried to stop the stampede when it had first begun.

Jessie could see the house clearly now, not more than seventy-five yards ahead. Breaking off, Jessie ran toward the side of the house. With any luck at all, the hired guns and hands would be in front or in back. She might be able to gain entrance around a side after the cattle had passed by.

She ran toward the barn, pressing herself flat against the wall as the cattle streamed by, not ten yards from her feet. Suddenly, the earth kicked up once between her boots. Then another shot splintered the wood a yard from her head. Looking up, Jessie saw Truesday, high up in a window of the house, a big rifle against her shoulder.

Jessie moved, crouching, as more shots followed her progress along the wall. Shooting back at the woman was useless. She'd have to take cover in the barn. Rounding the corner, she got to the door and slipped into the cool darkness.

No sooner was she inside than a flash broke the dark calm and a shotgun thundered.

Jessie brought the rifle up and fired. Another shotgun blast exploded in front of her as she dove for a stall.

"You damn woman, look what you did!" a voice called from the darkness. A second later, she heard the unmistakable sound of a shotgun breaking and then clicking together again.

Jessie fired toward the sound and heard footsteps running away into the darkness.

"You're not afraid of a woman, are you?" she called. "Someone told me Glamis was only hiring real men for this piece of work. Real men aren't afraid of a woman, are they?"

"Hell no," came the answer. " 'Fraid of that gun."

Jessie brought her head up over the railing and triggered off a shot toward the voice at the far end of the barn.

Another blast from the scattergun answered her

shot. But this time she saw where it came from. He was in a stall at the far end of the barn.

Slowly, Jessie crouched down and inched along the railing. The gunman had her at a disadvantage, she being backlit somewhat by the open door. She had to force his hand, otherwise he could keep her pinned down in the barn all night.

Jacking a shell into the chamber, she drew a deep breath and jumped into the open, diving and rolling to the opposite stall. The shotgun exploded and two feet from her head the birdshot kicked up the dirt and hay on the floor.

Now she had a clear idea of where he was. Coming up in a crouch, she fired and kept on firing until she'd run through four rounds. Off in the distance, she heard the panicked cry of horses, then a pained curse. She'd hit him, but didn't know how badly. Only now, there wasn't a choice.

She came out of her crouch and ran back toward her adversary firing as fast as she could. When the gun would no longer fire, she stopped. The barn was eerily quiet.

"You still there?" she called.

Nobody answered.

Jessie reloaded the rifle, then waited for what seemed like a long time. When she could wait no longer, she rose and walked slowly through into the barn, keeping close to the stalls, her finger ready to squeeze the trigger.

When she reached the last stall, she found the gunman. He'd been hit twice. The first one caught him in the elbow of his left arm, blowing it out into his gut. She knew this was the first shot, because from what she could see, the second had caught him in the right eye and had taken off most of the side of his head.

Jessie emerged from the barn carefully, bringing the rifle around the corner first. The stampede had all but ended. Only a few cattle remained, milling around the house. But they'd done their work. All around were the trampled bodies of the hired guns Glamis had brought to the ranch. It looked like a battlefield.

Shots sounded from the house and were answered by gunfire from close by. Jessie guessed that a few of the hired guns had made it to the house and were holding off Cawdor, Rosalie, and Ki. Peering up to that upstairs window, she searched for signs of Truesday, but saw none. The woman may have been dead, but Jessie doubted it.

Ducking back into the darkness of the barn, Jessie ran through to the opposite door. She came out again, moving quickly along the barn's wall. It was a hundred yards at a straight run to the side of the house. Once she reached it, she could climb in a side window.

She ran as fast as she could, not drawing any fire. It wasn't until she reached the side of the building that she saw Cawdor. He was crouching behind a bale of hay directly in the line of fire from the back windows. Rosalie, Jessie guessed, was the one firing from behind an overturned wagon, fifteen yards to Cawdor's left.

Jessie caught Cawdor's attention as he was reloading. Using hand signals, she made clear her intention of climbing in the side window. She hoped he knew what he had to do, which was keep

the gunmen in the house busy with a steady stream
of bullets.

Jessie reloaded from the gunbelt around her waist
and heard Cawdor yell to the person behind the
wagon. Rosalie popped her head up and six shots
slammed into the wagon's bed perilously close.

Drawing a deep breath, Jessie moved toward the
nearest window. Shots began to sound and she
watched as Cawdor ran out from behind the hay
bale and took cover behind a lone cow who had
somehow strayed into the crossfire. Beating the
cow on the rump, he moved it left, toward Rosalie's
position.

Jessie didn't have time to think about what he had
planned; she just hoped that Rosalie would keep the
gunmen's attention on them. Lifting herself up and
wiggling into the window, Jessie dropped lightly into
what was once the parlor. The place was a mess of
spent shells and liquor bottles. The hired guns had
not been kind to the Birnam house.

She walked down the hall toward the front of the
house. Three guns she figured, one for each window.
She didn't like shooting men in the back, but if it
came to that, then she would.

As she approached the kitchen, she saw them.
They were crouching beneath and to the sides of
the windows. All three had repeaters in their hands
and large cases of shells at their feet. If need be, they
could hold off an army.

Primitive animal instinct brought two of the
gunmen spinning on their heels as Jessie took two
steps into the room.

Jessie fired off two fast rounds from the hip as they
brought their rifles toward her. The first fell, as the

big slug tore away his ankle, the gun clattering to the floor. Shifting the rifle quickly to her shoulder, she shot the second an instant before he managed to squeeze off a round. The bullet whistled past Jessie's gunbelt and slammed into the wall.

Shifting the rifle slightly, Jessie fired again, and the hammer came down with a click, the cartridge misfiring.

The gunman smiled, rising up from his crouch as he held the rifle out in front of him. "Well, I just might have myself a pretty chip to play this poker game with," he snarled. "Now throw down that damned gun!"

Jessie turned the rifle in her hands, offering it to him butt first. "Take it," she said.

"I believe that's just what I'll do," he said, and took a step toward the rifle.

But a step was all it took for him to frame himself in the shattered window. A second later there was a shot and he pitched forward, a bullet in his back.

Jessie pulled the rifle back and grabbed his gun before he hit the floor, groaning.

"Sorry way to die, making a dumb-ass mistake like that," the gunman said, then died.

An instant later, Cawdor broke in through the door, rifle ready to shoot. "Looks like you got 'em all," he said, smiling.

"Not that last one," Jessie answered.

"Must have been Rosalie."

They walked cautiously through the house, moving from room to room. Everywhere were liquor bottles and bullets. As they approached the front parlor, they found Ki, moving toward them. Just behind him, in the parlor, were four dead men.

The three of them made their way up the stairs slowly. The house was silent. Whatever gunmen survived the stampede and shoot-out had no doubt fled. Walking from room to room they found the entire place deserted. There was no sign of Glamis or his wife.

"Looks like they got away clean," Jessie said.

They were coming down the stairs when they heard Rosalie cry out. She was yelling, "Here! Here!"

The sound of her voice froze the three of them in their tracks. Her cries weren't coming from the back of the house, but the front. Then, all at once they ran, taking the stairs two at a time.

When they reached the front door, they bolted through. There was Rosalie, gun in her hand, staring up at the roof and pointing.

Looking up, Jessie saw her. Truesday had positioned herself at the highest peak of the roof. In her hand was a cut-glass bottle. She was holding it to her mouth, drinking.

"What's that she's drinking?" Cawdor asked.

"Looks like perfume," Jessie said marveling at the sight. The last rays of the sun caught the bottle, turning the glass and its contents a blood red.

"Truesday, you come on down here, directly!" Cawdor yelled.

"You bastards!" the woman shouted back, staggering along the peaked roof. "This here is French perfume!"

"Well, quit drinking it then!" Cawdor called.

"They're coming," the woman shouted back and took another swig from the bottle. "You see 'em, they're coming!"

Turning, Jessie did see them. Four riders, maybe

155

five, coming up the road fast. She could tell, even from the distance, that they were Texas Rangers. "She can set them straight," Jessie whispered to Cawdor. "Tell them what happened."

"Truesday, you get yourself down here," Cawdor shouted as he nodded toward Jessie.

"Get her to come down," Rosalie pleaded.

"You listening to me?" Cawdor asked in a shout.

"I can hear you, but I ain't listening," Truesday shouted back. "I do believe I'll have myself another drink!" And she did, taking a long swallow of the fragrant poison.

"There's faster ways of killing yourself than drinking perfume," Cawdor tried. "Now, come on down here."

The woman took another drink and said, "If I come down, will you promise me something?"

"Sure, anything," Cawdor said. "What kind of promise you want?"

"You gotta promise to bury me in Philadelphia!" came the strange request.

As Jessie, Ki, Cawdor, and Rosalie looked at each other in disbelief, Truesday started gagging, the effects of the poison taking hold.

"Sure, Philadelphia," Cawdor said.

"Fine then," Truesday answered.

They watched, and for a moment Truesday did nothing. Then she jumped, her body sailing off the roof into the dirt.

Truesday was dead before the Rangers were within five hundred yards.

★

Chapter 15

Jessie knew that no amount of talking to the governor or anyone else could keep her arrest by the Rangers from happening. She had, after all, broken out of a jail, escaped from the Rangers at Delgado's ranch, stampeded a herd, and killed at least seven men.

As the Rangers drew near, all four of them slowly placed their guns on the ground and awaited the worst. Then, they saw Miranda riding abreast of the Ranger. She was sitting high in the saddle and smiling. A moment later, they recognized another face, that of Glamis. He was riding just behind the first two lawmen and Miranda. His hands were tied in front of him and he was not smiling.

"Lord almighty, what did you folks do here?" the first lawman called out.

More men emerged over the hill. Three more Rangers brought four prisoners walking alongside.

"Taking back my ranch," Cawdor answered.

"We picked up these folks down the road a bit,"

said the lead Ranger, whom Jessie now recognized as the man Cawdor fell on. "Been right talkative. Especially after I pointed out that the names on those statements those other hands signed were aliases attached to wanted men. Every last one had a price on his head."

"You believe us now, is that what you're telling us?" Cawdor asked, incredulously.

"Believe someone," the lawman answered, coming down slowly off his horse. "I think I'd like to believe you rather than a pack of murdering scum."

Glamis just sat on the horse, staring. Not even the sight of his wife's body moved him.

"How'd she die?" the Ranger asked, pointing to Truesday's body in the dirt, a shattered perfume bottle lying nearby.

"Drank about a quart of French perfume and jumped off the roof," Rosalie answered.

"Well, that's just as good a way as any, I suppose," the Ranger drawled.

It took more than three weeks just to collect the cattle. The herd was scattered over twenty miles. But it was good work, and Jessie enjoyed it.

Cawdor healed quickly. Nothing he had done to take back his ranch had helped the shoulder any, but somehow he'd managed to get back in the saddle within two weeks.

"You sure you're not going to stay for the trial?" Cawdor asked. "Another two weeks, that's when the judge comes back through town."

"I know," Jessie answered. "But I figure you got yourself enough witnesses. Half dozen Rangers, can't ask for better witnesses than that in Texas."

"Gonna come back for the hanging, then?" he asked, already knowing the answer.

"Can't say I care much for them."

"Even a son of a bitch like Glamis?"

"Even a son of a bitch like him," Jessie replied. "Never liked them much."

Suddenly Cawdor's mood turned serious. Jessie could sense it, without him saying a word. "You have something you want to get out?" she asked.

Then he hemmed and hawed like a schoolboy, almost getting to the point of scratching his toe in the dirt. "Jessica Starbuck, you are just flat-out one helluva woman," he said at last.

They were off in a far pasture, their horses hitched to the fence wire as they mended fence in the afternoon's fading light.

"Well, I just appreciate that, Cawdor," Jessie answered, stretching the wire tight. "Now if you'll be so kind as get those nails in, maybe we can get some supper tonight."

"No, I mean it," he said, fastening the wire to the post. "Mean it like I never meant anything before."

Jessie released the wire. "I know it," she said, turning serious for his sake. "What're you planning now?"

"I got a good cook in Rosalie," Cawdor answered, finishing the job.

"Got to sign on some hands," Jessie said, and started back to the horses.

"I was thinking about starting with that Kramer boy," Cawdor said.

"Thought he'd be halfway past Mexico by now," Jessie answered.

"Got a wire yesterday when I was in town," Cawdor

said. "He's down at Delgado's talking the old man's ear off. They wanted to know what they should do with him."

Jessie climbed into the saddle. "You're gonna take him to raise, are you?"

"Well, I suppose I could send him down your way," Cawdor answered. "He's a strong lad, needs a job bad."

"That he does," Jessie answered, and spurred her horse in the direction of the house before Cawdor could answer.

Watch for

**LONE STAR
AND THE MONTANA MARAUDERS**

140th novel in the exciting LONE STAR series
from Jove

Coming in April!

SPECIAL PREVIEW!

One was a Yankee gentleman, the other a Rebel hellraiser. They met in a barroom brawl, and the only thing they had in common was a price on their heads—and an aversion to honest work . . .

Texas Horsetrading Co.

Gene Shelton, acclaimed author of *Texas Legends,* brings you a rousing new epic novel of the Wild West.

*Here is a special excerpt
from this authentic new Western
—available from Diamond Books . . .*

The last thing Brubs McCallan remembered was a beer bottle headed straight for the bridge of his nose.

Now he came awake in a near panic, a cold, numbing fear that he had gone blind. Beyond the stabbing pain in his head he could make out only jerky, hazy shapes.

Brubs sighed with relief as he realized he was only in jail.

The shapes were hazy and indistinct partly because only a thin, weak light filtered into the cell from the low flame of a guttering oil lamp on a shelf outside the bars. And the shapes were fuzzy partly because his left eye was swollen almost shut.

Brubs leaned back against the thin blankets on the hard wooden cot and groaned. The movement sent the sledgehammer in his head to pounding a fresh set of spikes through his temples.

"Good morning."

Brubs started at the sound of the voice. He tried to focus his good eye on the dim form on the cot across the room. He could tell that the man was tall. His boots stuck out past the end of the cot. He had an arm hooked behind his head for a pillow, his hat pulled down over his eyes. "Mornin' yourself," Brubs mumbled over a swollen lower lip. "Question is, which mornin' is it, anyway?"

"Sunday, I believe. How do you feel?"

"Like I had a boot hung up in the stirrup and got drug over half of Texas." Brubs lifted a hand to his puffy face and heard the scratch of his palm against stubble. "And like somebody swabbed the outhouse with my tongue. Other than that, passin' fair."

"Glad to hear that. I was afraid that beer bottle might have caused some permanent damage."

Brubs swung his feet over the edge of the cot, sat up, and immediately regretted it. The hammer slammed harder against the spikes in his brain. He squinted at the tall man on the bunk across the way. "I remember you," he said after a moment. "How come you whopped me with that beer bottle?"

"I couldn't find an ax handle and you were getting the upper hand on me at the time," the man said.

Brubs wiggled his nose between a thumb and forefinger. "At least you didn't bust my beak again," he said. "That would have plumb made me mad. I done broke it twice the last year and a half. What was we fightin' about?"

The tall man swung his feet over the side of the cot and sat, rubbing a hand across the back of his neck. "You don't remember? After all, you started it."

"Oh. Yeah, I reckon it's comin' back now. But that

166

cowboy was cheatin'. Seen him palm a card on his deal." Brubs snorted in disgust. "Wasn't even good at cheatin'."

"How do you know that?"

"If he'd been any good I wouldn't of caught him. I can't play poker worth a flip. Who pulled him off me?"

"I did."

"What'd you do that for? I had him right where I wanted him. I was hittin' him square in the fist with my face ever' time he swung. Another minute or two, I'd of had him wore plumb down."

"I didn't want to interfere, but I saw him reach for a knife. That didn't seem fair in a fistfight."

Brubs sighed. "You're dead right about that. That when I belted you?"

"The first time."

Brubs heaved himself unsteadily to his feet. It wasn't easy. Brubs packed a hundred and sixty pounds of mostly muscle on a stubby five-foot-seven frame, and it seemed to him that every one of those muscles was bruised, stretched, or sore. Standing up didn't help his head much, either.

The man on the other bunk raised a hand. "If you don't mind, I'd just as soon not start it again. I don't have a beer bottle with me at the moment."

"Aw, hell," Brubs said, "I wasn't gonna start nothin'. Just wanted to say I'm obliged you didn't let that cowboy stick a knife in my gizzard." He strode stiffly to the side of the bunk and offered a hand. "Brubs McCallan."

The man on the cot stood. He was a head taller than Brubs, lean and wiry, built along the lines of a mountain cat where Brubs tended toward the badger clan. The lanky man took Brubs's hand. His grip was firm and dry. "Dave Willoughby. Nice to make your acquaintance under more civilized conditions."

"Wouldn't call the San Antonio jail civilized," Brubs said with a grin. The smile started his split lower lip to leaking blood again. He released Willoughby's hand. "We tear the place up pretty good?"

"My last recollection is that we had made an impressive start to that end," Willoughby said. "Shortly thereafter, somebody blew the lantern out on me, too."

Both men turned as a door creaked open and bootsteps sounded. The oil lamp outside the cell flared higher as a stocky man twisted the brass key of the wick feeder with a thick hand. The light spilled over a weathered face crowned by an unruly thatch of gray hair. "What's all the yammering about? Gettin' so a man can't sleep around here anymore."

The stocky man stood with the lamp held at shoulder height. A ring of keys clinked as he hobbled to the cell. His left knee was stiff. He had to swing the leg in a half circle when he walked. The lamplight glittered from a badge on his vest and the brass back strap of a big revolver holstered high on his right hip.

"You the sheriff?" Brubs asked.

"Night deputy. Sheriff don't come on duty for another couple hours. Name's Charlie Purvis. If you boys are gonna be the guests of Bexar County for a while, you better learn to keep it quiet when I'm on duty."

"We will certainly keep that in mind, Deputy Purvis," Dave Willoughby said. "We apologize for having disturbed you. We will be more reserved in the future."

Brubs glared through his one open eye at the deputy. "What do you mean, guests of the county?"

"In case you boys ain't heard," the deputy said, "that brawl you started over at the Longhorn just about wrecked the place. I don't figure you two've got enough to pay the fines and damages."

Dave sighed audibly. "How much might that be, Deputy?"

"Twenty-dollar fine apiece for startin' the fight and disturbin' the peace. Thirty-one dollars each for damages. Plus a dime for the beer bottle you busted over your friend's head."

"What?" Brubs's voice was a startled croak. "You gonna charge this man a dime for whoppin' me with a beer bottle?"

The deputy shrugged. "Good glass bottles are hard to find out here. Owner of the Longhorn says they're worth a dime apiece."

Brubs snorted in disgust. "Damnedest thing I ever heard." He glanced up at Willoughby. "Good thing you didn't hit me with the back bar mirror. God knows what that would of cost. You got any money, Dave?"

Willoughby rummaged in a pocket and poked a finger among a handful of coins. "Thirty-one cents."

Brubs sighed in relief. "Good. There for a minute I was afraid we was plumb broke." He fumbled in his own pocket. "I got seventeen cents. Had four dollars when I set in on that poker game."

"Looks like you boys got troubles," Purvis said, shaking his shaggy head. "Can't let you out till the fines and damages are paid."

169

"How we gonna pay if we're in jail?"

Purvis shrugged. "Should have thought about that before you decided to wreck the Longhorn. Guess you'll just have to work it out on the county farm."

"Farm!" Brubs sniffed in wounded indignation and held out his hands. "These look like farmer's hands?"

The deputy squinted. "Nope. Don't show no sign of work if you don't count the skinned knuckles." Purvis grinned. "They'll toughen up quick on a hoe handle. We got forty acres in corn and cotton, and ten weeds for every crop plant. Pay's four bits a day." He scratched his jaw with a thick finger. "Let's see, now—fifty cents a day, you owe fifty-one dollars . . . Works out to a hundred and two days. Each."

Dave Willoughby sighed. "Looks like it's going to be a long summer."

Purvis plucked a watch from his vest pocket, flipped the case open, and grunted. "Near onto sunup. You boys wrecked my nap. Might as well put some coffee on." He snapped the watch shut. "I reckon the county can spare a couple cups if you two rowdies want some."

Brubs scrubbed a hand over the back of his neck. "I'll shoot anybody you want for a cup of coffee. Got anything for hangovers? I got a size twelve headache in a size seven head."

The deputy chuckled. "Sympathy's all I got to offer. Know how you feel. I been there, back in my younger days. Busted up a saloon or two myself. You boys sit tight. I'll be back in a few minutes with the coffee."

Brubs trudged back to the cot and sat, elbows propped against his knees. He became aware of a gray light spreading through the cell and glanced at the wall above Dave's bunk. A small, barred rectangle high above the floor brightened with the approaching dawn. "Well, Dave," Brubs said after a moment, "you sure got us in a mess this time."

Willoughby turned to face Brubs, a quizzical expression on his face. "*I* got us in a mess? I was under the impression that you started the fight and I was the innocent bystander."

Brubs shrugged as best he could without moving his throbbing head. "Don't matter. Question now is, how do we break out of here?"

Willoughby raised a hand, palm out. "Wait a minute—you can't be serious! Breaking out of jail is a felony offense. We would be wanted criminals, possibly with a price on our heads. If you're thinking of escape, even if it was possible, count me out."

Brubs prodded his puffy eyebrow with a finger. The swelling seemed to be going down some. "I ain't working for the county, Dave. 'Specially not on some damn farm." He squinted at his free hand. "These hands don't fit no hoe handle. That's how come I left home in the first place."

Willoughby strode to his own bunk and stretched out on his back. "Where's home?"

"Nacogdoches, I reckon. Never had a real home to call it such." He raised his undamaged eyebrow at Willoughby. "You sure talk funny. Since we're tradin' life stories here, where you from?"

"Cincinnati."

"That on the Sabine or the Red River?"

"Neither. It's on the Ohio."

Brubs moaned. "Oh, Christ. I'm sittin' here tryin' my best to die from day-old whiskey, I got my butt whupped in a saloon fight, I owe money I ain't got,

171

I been threatened with choppin' cotton, and now it turns out I'm sharin' a room with a Yankee. If I hadn't had such a damn good time last night, I'd be plumb disgusted."

A faint smile flitted over Willoughby's face. "I suppose it was a rather interesting diversion, at that." He winced and probed the inside of his cheek with his tongue. "I think you chipped one of my teeth. For a little man, you swing a mean punch."

The creak of the door between cell block and outer office brought both men to their feet. Brubs could smell the coffee before the deputy came into view, carrying two tin cups on a flat wooden slab. Purvis crouched stiffly and slid the cups through the grub slot of the cell.

Brubs grabbed a cup, scorched his fingers on the hot tin, sipped at the scalding liquid, and sighed, contented. "Mother's milk for a hungover child," he said. "If I was a preacher I'd bless your soul, Charlie Purvis."

Purvis straightened slowly, the creak of his joints clearly audible. "You boys'll get some half-raw bacon and burnt biscuits when the sheriff gets here. Need anything else meantime?"

"I don't reckon you could see your way clear to leave the key in the lock?" Brubs asked hopefully.

Purvis shook his head. "Couldn't do that." He pointed toward a dark smear on the adobe wall near the door of the office. "Just in case you boys got some ideas perkin' along with the headaches, study on that spot over there. That's what's left of the last man tried to bust out of my jail." He clucked his tongue. "Sure did hate to cut down on him with that smoothbore. Double load of buckshot

172

splattered guts all over the place. Made a downright awful mess. Why, pieces of that fellow were—"

"I think we understand your message, Deputy," Willoughby interrupted with a wince. "If you don't mind, spare us the gory details."

The deputy shrugged. "Well, I'll leave you boys to your chicken pluckin'. Sure don't envy you none. It gets hotter than the devil's kitchen out in those fields in summer."

Brubs moaned aloud at the comment.

"Is there somebody who could help us?" Willoughby asked. "A bondsman, perhaps, or someone who would loan us the money to get out of here?"

Charlie Purvis frowned. "Might be one man. I'm not sure you'd like the deal, though."

"Charlie," Brubs said, pleading, "I'd make a deal with Old Scratch himself to keep my hands off a damn hoe handle."

The deputy shrugged. "Same difference, maybe. But I'll talk to him." Purvis turned and limped away. The door creaked shut behind him.

Brubs stopped pacing the narrow cell and glanced at the small, high window overhead, then at the lean man reclining on the bunk. "How long we been in this place, Dave?"

Willoughby shoved the hat back from over his eyes. "I'd guess a little over half a day."

"Seems a passel longer than that."

"Patience, I gather, is not your strong suit."

Brubs snorted. "Buzzards got patience. All it gets 'em is rotten meat and a yard and a half of ugly apiece." He started pacing again.

"Relax, Brubs," Willoughby said, "you're wasting

173

energy and tiring me out, tromping back and forth like that." He pulled the hat back over his eyes. "Better save your strength for that cotton patch."

Brubs paused to glare at the man on the cot. "You are truly a comfort to a dyin' man, Dave Willoughby. Truly a comfort."

The clomp of boots and the squeak of the door brought Brubs's pacing to a halt. Sheriff Milt Garrison strode to the cell, a big, burly man at his side. The big man seemed to wear more hair than a grizzly, Brubs thought. Gray fur covered most of his face, bristled his forearms, sprouted from heavy knuckles, and even stuck out through the buttonholes on his shirt. For a moment Brubs thought the man didn't have eyes. Then he realized they were the same color as the hair and were tucked back under brows as thick and wiry as badger bristles.

"These the two Charlie told me about?" The hairy man's voice grated like a shovel blade against gravel.

"That's them." Milt Garrison leaned against the bars of the cell. "Told you they didn't look like much."

"Well, hell," the hairy one said, "if they're tough enough to wreck the Longhorn, maybe they'll do."

"Boys, meet Lawrence T. Pettibone, owner of Bexar and Rio Grande Freight Lines. He's got a deal to offer you." Garrison waved a hand toward the prisoners. "The short one's Brubs McCallan. Other one's Dave Willoughby."

Lawrence T. Pettibone nodded a greeting. "I hear you boys run up a pretty big bill last night. How bad you want to get shut of this place?"

174

"Mighty bad, Mr. Pettibone," Brubs said.

"All right, here's the deal. I won't say it but once, so you listen careful." Pettibone's smoky eyes seemed to turn harder, like a prize agate marble Brubs remembered from his childhood. "I need two men. You boys got horses and saddles?"

Brubs nodded. "Yes, sir, Mr. Pettibone, we sure do. Over at the livery."

Pettibone snorted. "Probably owe money on them, too."

"Yes, sir. I reckon we owe a dollar apiece board on the mounts."

"You savvy guns?"

Brubs nodded again. "Sure do. I'm a better'n fair hand with a long gun, and I can hit an outhouse with a pistol if it ain't too far off."

"How about you, Willoughby?"

Willoughby's brow wrinkled. "Yes, sir, I can use weapons. If the need arises." His tone sounded cautious.

Pettibone grunted. Brubs couldn't tell if it was a good grunt or a bad grunt. "All right, I guess you two'll do. I was hopin' for better, but a man can't be too picky these days." He pulled a twist of tobacco from a shirt pocket, gnawed off a chew, and settled it in his cheek. "I need two outriders. Guards for a shipment goin' to El Paso day after tomorrow. I'll pay your fines and damages. You ride shotgun for the Bexar and Rio line until you work it off. At a dollar a day."

Brubs sighed in relief. "Dave, that's twice the pay the county offered. And no hoe handles."

"Mr. Pettibone," Willoughby said, "may I inquire as to why you are short of manpower?"

Pettibone twisted his head and spat a wad of tobacco juice. It spanged neatly into a brass cuspidor below the lamp shelf. "Bandits killed 'em last run. Blew more holes in 'em than we could count. Stole my whole damn load."

"Bandits? You mean outlaws?"

Pettibone sighed in disgust. "Now just who the hell else would hold up a freight wagon? A gang of Methodist preachers?"

Willoughby shook his head warily. "I'm not sure about this, Mr. Pettibone. It's one thing to work for a man. It's another matter to possibly have to kill or be killed in the line of work."

Pettibone's gray eyes narrowed. "Suit yourself, son. It don't matter to me. But I need *two* men. Charlie said he figured you two come as a package. Guess I'll have to find me a couple other saddle tramps." He turned and started to walk away.

"Mr. Pettibone, wait a minute," Brubs called. He turned to Dave. "You leave the talkin' to me, Dave," he whispered. "I'm gettin' out of here, and you're goin' with me."

The big man turned back.

"My partner here ain't no lace-drawers type, Mr. Pettibone," Brubs said earnestly. "He's a top hand with a gun and got more guts than a bull buffalo. He just went through some stuff in the war that bothers him time to time. Don't you fret about old Dave." He clapped his cell mate on the shoulder. "You just get us out of here, and we'll make sure your wagon gets through."

Pettibone glared at the two prisoners for several heartbeats, then shrugged. "All right. You're hired." He jabbed a heavy finger at Brubs. "I want you boys

176

to know one thing. I ain't in the charity business. You duck out or turn yellow on me and you'll wish to high hell you were back in this lockup, 'cause I'll skin you out and tan your hides for a pillow to ease my piles, and every time I go to the outhouse I'll take it along to remember you by. Savvy?"

"Yes, sir," Brubs said eagerly, "we savvy. You're the boss."

"Good. Keep that in mind. I'll pick you boys up tomorrow afternoon." He turned to walk away.

"Mr. Pettibone?"

"Now what, McCallan?"

Brubs swallowed. "Reckon you could get us out today? No disrespect to Bexar County or this fine sheriff here, but this ain't the most comfortable jail I ever been in. I sure would like to get my stuff in shape and take the kinks out of my sorrel before we move out."

Pettibone glowered at Brubs for a moment. "Damned if you boys don't try a man's patience something fierce. All right, I'll get you out now. You got any place to stay?"

"No, sir, Mr. Pettibone."

Pettibone's massive chest rose and fell. Brubs thought he saw the hair in the big man's ears bristle. "You can bunk in at my place. Cost you a dollar a day apiece. I'll add it onto what it's going to cost me to spring the pair of you. Damn, but the cost of help's gettin' high these days." Pettibone turned to the sheriff. "Cut 'em loose, Milt."

Brubs heaved a deep sigh of relief as the key turned in the cell lock and the barred door swung open. He knew it was the same air outside the cell as in, but it still smelled better. He and Willoughby fell into step behind the sheriff and Pettibone.

Brubs and Willoughby waited patiently as Lawrence T. Pettibone frowned at the column of figures on Sheriff Milt Garrison's ledger. "What the hell's this ten cents for a beer bottle?"

"Dave busted one over my head, Mr. Pettibone," Brubs said.

Pettibone snorted in disgust. "Damnedest thing I ever heard," he growled. "Chargin' a man for bustin' a beer bottle in a saloon brawl."

"Sort of the way I figured it, Mr. Pettibone," Brubs said earnestly. "Pricin' a man's fun plumb out of sight these days."

"I ain't payin' for no damn bottle," Pettibone said. "No way I can figure how to get ten cents' worth of work out of two guys on a dollar a day."

Brubs dug in a pocket and produced a coin. "Give me a nickel, Dave. We'll split the cost of the bottle."

Pettibone finally grunted and pulled a wad of bills from a pocket. Brubs's eyes went wide at the sight of the roll. It was more money than he'd seen in one place since the big horse race up in Denton. Pettibone licked a thumb and counted out the bills, sighing as he caressed each one. Pettibone acted like he was burying a sainted mother every time he put a dollar on the desk, Brubs thought.

Garrison gathered up the bills, dropped the money in a tin box, and scribbled a receipt. He handed the paper to Pettibone, then retrieved the prisoners' weapons from a locked closet. "Guess you bought yourself some shotgun riders, Lawrence," he said.

Pettibone cast a cold glance at Brubs and Willoughby. "Don't know if I bought a good horse or a wind-broke plug," he groused. "I sure as hell hope they ride and shoot better than they smell. You boys are a touch ripe. There's a big water tank out by my wagon barn. Wouldn't hurt either of you to nuzzle up to some soap. Now, strap them gun belts on and let's go bail your horses out of the lockup."

Willoughby paused for a moment, rotated the cylinder of his Colt, and raised an eyebrow. "Should we go ahead and load the chambers now, Mr. Pettibone?" he asked.

Pettibone groaned aloud. "Fools. I just bought two idiots with my hard-earned money. Dammit, son, what good's an unloaded pistol?" He watched in disgust as Willoughby thumbed cartridges into the Colt and reached for his Winchester rifle. "I guess you boys got plenty of ammunition?"

"I got ten rifle cartridges," Brubs said, shoving loads into his scarred Henry .44 rimfire long gun. "Maybe a dozen for the pistol."

"I have half a box of .44-40's," Willoughby said. "Same caliber fits both my handgun and rifle."

Pettibone snorted in disgust. "Damn. Now I've got to lay out some more hard cash on you two. My men don't ride with less than a hundred rounds each. Come on—we'll stop off at the general store down the street."

The two men fell into step behind Pettibone. A few minutes later the hairy one emerged from the store, four boxes of ammunition in a big hand. "I'll add the cost of the shells to your bill, boys. Fifty cents a box."

"Fifty cents? Mr. Pettibone, that's a dime more than I paid anywhere," Brubs said, incredulous.

"Call it a nuisance fee," Pettibone growled,

"because you boys are nuisances if I ever seen 'em. Course, if you'd rather work it out with the county—"

"No, sir," Brubs said quickly. "I reckon that's fair enough. We won't nuisance you no more."

"I doubt that." Pettibone spat a wad of used-up tobacco into the street. "Let's get home before you two drifters cost me my last dollar."

"Mr. Pettibone?"

"What now, McCallan?"

"Any chance we could get a bottle of whiskey added to our bill?"

"No, by God!" Pettibone bellowed. "Don't push your luck, boy, or you'll be behind a hoe handle all summer!"

"Yes, sir," Brubs said. "But it was worth a try."

A half hour later, Brubs and Willoughby rode side by side behind Lawrence T. Pettibone's buggy. Brubs forked a big, rangy sorrel, and Dave rode a leggy black that looked to have some Tennessee racing stock in his bloodline.

"Brubs," Willoughby said quietly, "I have the distinct impression that our new employer is somewhat thrifty with his funds."

Brubs flashed a quick grin. "I reckon he can squeeze a peso until the Mexican eagle looks like a plucked crow."

Lawrence T. Pettibone's combination home and wagon yard and adjoining stock pastures spread over most of a section on the northern outskirts of San Antonio.

Brubs had to admit he was impressed. The corrals were sturdy, fenced by peeled logs the size of a man's thigh, and watered by a big windmill that creaked as it whirred in the southwest breeze. The barn was as solidly built as the corrals, expansive and well-ventilated. The main house was big, and built of real cut lumber, not adobe or split logs.

Brubs was even more impressed with what came from inside the big house.

Pettibone pushed the door open, growled at Brubs and Willoughby to wait on the porch, and went inside. He was back a minute later with a stiff-bristled brush and a bar of lye soap in hand, and one of the prettiest girls Brubs had seen west of Savannah trailing behind.

The girl was blonde. Palomino hair tumbled past her shoulders, dancing gold in the warm afternoon sunshine. The pale rose housedress she wore wrapped itself around a figure that made Brubs want to paw the ground and snort. Her eyes were big, blue, and had a smoldering look about them above a perky, upturned nose. She looked to be about twenty. This, Brubs knew instinctively, was one hot-blooded woman. He swept the battered and stained hat from his head.

"Boys, this here is Callie, my daughter," Pettibone said. "Callie, these two bums'll be riding shotgun for us a spell. Don't shoot 'em for prowlers until I get my money back out of 'em. The little feller's name is Brubs McCallan. The tall one's Dave Willoughby."

Brubs bowed deep at the waist, then grinned at the blonde. He wished for a moment he had just had a bath and shave; some women were mighty picky about that, as if it made some sort of difference. "Mighty pleased to make your acquaintance, Miss

Pettibone," Brubs said. "A pretty girl does brighten a poor saddle tramp's day."

"Lay a hand on Callie and I'll kill you," Pettibone said. It wasn't exactly a threat, Brubs noted. More like a statement of fact.

Brubs tore his gaze from the girl and glanced at his cell mate. Willoughby had removed his hat, but merely nodded a greeting. He did not speak.

A second woman, a Mexican somewhere in her late twenties, appeared at the door. She was a bit thick of hip and waist, her upper lip dusted by scattered but distinct black hairs. Overall, though, not bad looking, Brubs decided. Away from the blonde she might even be pretty.

"That's Juanita. She's the cook and maid." Pettibone held out the brush and lye soap. "Long as I'm makin' introductions, this is stuff to clean up with. Put your horses in the barn and yourselves in that water tank out back, or don't come in for supper."

Brubs hesitated, reluctant to leave the warm glow that seemed to spread in all directions from Callie, until he realized that Lawrence T. Pettibone was glaring a hole through him. Brubs quickly replaced his hat, turned away, and mounted with a flourish, swinging into the saddle without touching a stirrup. He wasn't above showing off a bit when a pretty girl was watching. He kneed his sorrel gelding around and set off after Willoughby, who was already leading his leggy black toward the barn thirty yards away.

"Man, ain't she something?" Brubs said as he reined in alongside Willoughby. "I ain't seen a filly like that my whole life through. Prime stuff, that Callie."

Willoughby cast a worried glance at Brubs. "You heard what Pettibone said, Brubs. You'd better leave the girl alone."

Brubs chuckled aloud. "Just adds a little spice to the puddin', my Yankee friend. You see the way Callie was lookin' at me? Her eyes got all smoky-like."

"I saw the way Pettibone was looking at you." Willoughby swung the corral gate open.

"Ah, that inflated tadpole ain't much to worry about," Brubs said.

"I worry about a lot of things, Brubs. One of which is that if you try messing around with that girl, somebody is likely to get hurt. Like you and me."

Brubs reached down and cuffed Dave on the shoulder. "Don't you fret, Dave. You just watch ol' Brubs work that herd, you'll learn somethin' about handlin' women."

"And that," Willoughby said solemnly, "is exactly what's bothering me. I'm beginning to wonder if perhaps Brubs McCallan wasn't put on this earth just to get one Dave Willoughby killed."

A special offer for people who enjoy reading the best Westerns published today.

WESTERNS!

NO OBLIGATION

Mail the coupon below

To start your subscription and receive 2 FREE WESTERNS, fill out the coupon below and mail it today. We'll send your first shipment which includes 2 FREE BOOKS as soon as we receive it.

Mail To: **True Value Home Subscription Services, Inc. P.O. Box 5235**
120 Brighton Road, Clifton, New Jersey 07015-5235

YES! I want to start reviewing the very best Westerns being published today. Send me my first shipment of 6 Westerns for me to preview FREE for 10 days. If I decide to keep them, I'll pay for just 4 of the books at the low subscriber price of $2.75 each; a total $11.00 (a $21.00 value). Then each month I'll receive the 6 newest and best Westerns to preview Free for 10 days. If I'm not satisfied I may return them within 10 days and owe nothing. Otherwise I'll be billed at the special low subscriber rate of $2.75 each; a total of $16.50 (at least a $21.00 value) and save $4.50 off the publishers price. There are never any shipping, handling or other hidden charges. I understand I am under no obligation to purchase any number of books and I can cancel my subscription at any time, no questions asked. In any case the 2 FREE books are mine to keep.

Name _____

Street Address _____ Apt. No. _____

City _____ State _____ Zip Code _____

Telephone _____

Signature _____
(if under 18 parent or guardian must sign)

Terms and prices subject to change. Orders subject
to acceptance by True Value Home Subscription
Services, Inc.

11339-5